more
than
good
enough

more than than

CRISSA-JEAN CHAPPELL

good enough

flux®

Woodbury, Minnesota

First Edition
First Printing, 2014

Book design by Bob Gaul
Cover design by Ellen Lawson
Cover image © Superstock/4107-620/Belinda Images

Flux, an imprint of Llewellyn Worldwide Ltd.

Library of Congress Cataloging-in-Publication Data
Chappell, Crissa-Jean.
  More than good enough/Crissa-Jean Chappell.—First edition.
      pages cm
  Summary: "When seventeen-year-old Trent Osceola moves to the Rez to live with his father, a member of Florida's Miccosukee Tribe, he faces new questions about his identity and reconnects with his childhood friend Pippa"—Provided by publisher.
  ISBN 978-0-7387-3644-0
1. Mikasuki Indians—Juvenile fiction. [1. Mikasuki Indians—Fiction. 2. Indians of North America—Florida—Fiction. 3. Indian reservations—Fiction. 4. Identity—Fiction. 5. Friendship—Fiction. 6. Florida—Fiction.] I. Title.
  PZ7.C37275Mo2014
  [Fic]—dc23
                                                              2013028526

Flux
Llewellyn Worldwide Ltd.
2143 Wooddale Drive
Woodbury, MN 55125-2989
www.fluxnow.com

Printed in the United States of America

for Harlan

one

Names are like tree rings. You might end up with a lot. But if you chopped me open and looked inside, you'd find only one. That's the first thing I learned after I moved onto the Miccosukee reservation with my dad.

We were gliding through the Everglades on Uncle Seth's airboat. The late afternoon sky gleamed in the smooth surface of the water, as if the clouds rolled under us. All around the boat, a chain of lilies floated. Nothing to hear except the fan blades roaring away.

On my lap, I held the baby alligator that we'd caught in the tall grass. My uncle said that somebody must've kept the gator as a pet. When it grew too big, they dumped it in the swamp.

"They probably kept him in a bathtub," he said, tapping the gator's snout. "He didn't eat right. Not enough meat and bones. See, his back's all twisted."

The gator squirmed in my fingers, looking for escape.

I knew how he felt.

We swerved up to the docks and cut the engine. A sign bolted to the post said *MICCOSUKEE PROPERTY. NO TRESPASSING.* The breeze smelled like woodsmoke and low tide. My aunts had waited for us all day, cooking *sofke* with cornbread.

Our sneakers clattered down the boardwalk. In the middle of the island was a chickee hut, its thatched roof jutting above the oak trees. No walls. Everybody was hanging out by the fire, talking super fast in *Hitchiti*. I didn't understand a single word, but I had a feeling it was about me. A bunch of kids were running around, playing stickball. They wore patchwork shirts that drooped over their jeans, and in both hands, they carried rackets. They took turns, lunging across the grass. I wanted to join them, but I had no clue how to play.

As I turned away, Dad called out, "Trent, aren't you hungry?"

"No," I said, heading to the water.

I found a quiet spot by the canal. Uncle Seth and my dad used to climb the big trees here, but that was a long time ago. Now the shoreline was choked with stringy cattails, the "gravestone" of the Everglades.

"A lot of fish have disappeared," my uncle said. "Back in the day, we had so many, they used to jump into my canoe."

I couldn't tell if he was making this up. Uncle Seth was real good at stretching the truth. Not that I'd call him a liar.

I mean, at least he didn't mess with my head. That was my dad's job.

In my arms, I held the gator. Did he even have a name? I crouched down near the canal and let go. Uncle Seth told me it couldn't survive on its own, but I didn't believe it. For a second, the gator didn't move. Then it crawled into the water like it knew exactly where it belonged.

A couple weeks before, I was in the garage at my mom's house, messing around with my bass guitar, trying to teach myself this epic spider-walk technique I learned on YouTube. It was sad how much I'd been neglecting my bass. My pinky kept slipping over the frets and making this wacked-out *zppppptttt* noise. It was beyond irritating.

Music is what got me into Southwinds, the magnet school for super-obsessed people who start playing violin at age two. Right. Everybody's a genius. Here's the truth. My grades had crashed and burned that last semester. I just wasn't into it. Not when you've got teachers like Mr. Harding (aka Hard On) forcing you to play *Canon in D* over and over. It was so freaking boring. If I tried to freestyle, he'd get pissed.

When Mom found out I'd been ejected from Southwinds, she blamed the school. Then she called the principal and he blamed me.

"How could you fail all your exams?" Mom wanted to know.

Easy. I never went to class.

"This is inexcusable, Trenton," she said, slamming down the phone. "I can't have you going to Palm Hammock with all those druggies. Lord, what is this world coming to? They're installing metal detectors on campus. I read it in the paper."

If you asked me, regular school sounded a hell of a lot better. Metal detectors were nothing major unless you're, like, carrying a Bowie knife in your sock.

Mom wouldn't drop it. "We are having a discussion. Now."

Discuss what? I was already done. Over and out.

I sank into the chair and slapped the tabs to "All Along the Watchtower." My dad used to say that Jimi Hendrix was part Cherokee. When I was little, Dad would lock himself in here and play along with 94.9 Zeta Rocks. He'd crank the stereo so nobody would catch his mistakes. Still, I could tell he was good. More than good.

Mom got so frustrated with my little solo, she left the garage. I think she started crying. I felt kind of guilty for a nanosecond. Then I heard her on the phone, talking to my dad. They got divorced when I was little and he spent the past decade behind bars, but now that he'd gotten out of jail, he was staying with us. He was supposed to be looking for work, but as far as I could tell that wasn't happening.

I played louder.

Jimi's refrain buzzed through me, as if his rage had channeled into my hands. That's the most awesome part about bass guitar. It's a physical thing, almost percussive. I was so into it, I didn't hear the car pull into the driveway.

The garage door rumbled open, ultra-dramatic. I watched a blade of light cut across the wall. In my mind, I heard drums thumping like the soundtrack to an old Western. I really hated those movies. The Indians were usually white people in headbands. The director would record their lines and play it backward, just to make it sound like another language. How dumb is that?

My dad marched up to me, wiggling his hands in the air. "Rocking out" on air guitar. Yeah, that's what he was doing. God, just kill me now.

"Very cool," he said. "How long you been playing?"

"About an hour," I said.

He looked confused, then gave me a fake-ass laugh. "No, I mean, when did you start taking lessons?"

Dad had never heard me play, but he's the one who'd promised to teach me. Obviously, that's hard to do behind bars. So Mom dragged me to Suniland Music, this place inside a strip mall. A player piano gleamed in the front window, the keys thudding all by themselves. Mom said it was "high class," but it always scared the shit out of me.

Dad tried again. "So, I hear you're switching schools. What's going on with that?" He scratched his goatee, one of his "very cool" props, in addition to the "awesome" cargo shorts and the "bling" around his neck. Yeah, he was living the thug life.

This whole situation was making me sick. Without saying anything, I picked up my skateboard and shoved past him. Dad was yelling at me. There wasn't much I could do about it. What did he want? I couldn't go back in time and change my grades.

I slammed the board on the concrete. God, I used to skate, like, the second I woke up on Saturdays. Now the deck was chipped and I needed to glue it back together. The bearings were gunked with dirt. Basically, I'd been abusing that board with neglect, just like the rest of my life.

As I rattled across the driveway, I made up lyrics in my head. Nothing that deserved an award. Just random phrases about the darkness, how it swallows you whole. Guess I was talking to myself. Pretty sad, I know.

The neighbors at the end of the block were really getting into Christmas. They had this massive palm tree in their yard. All the fronds sparkled with plastic snowflakes. It must've taken them forever to decorate it. At that moment, I couldn't decide if I admired their efforts or thought they were balls-to-the-wall crazy. Maybe both.

Somebody had plunked a Dixie cup onto one of the lower branches. This made me so mad, I rolled over there and snatched it up. Then I didn't know what to do with it. I kept skating until finally I just left it in this lady's mailbox. She was mean, anyway. One time, she called the cops because I was playing my bass at night. It wasn't even that late, but old people have no concept of time. They're always sleeping.

When I got back, the garage smelled like bacon grease,

this morning's leftovers. Mom hadn't even started making dinner. A bad sign. I dumped my board near the door and barged inside. Dad was sitting on the couch with Mom. Even worse, he had his arm around her, like she was his personal possession. I watched him blink and knew he was telling some bullshit story.

"...needs to learn how to restructure his time," Dad was saying.

I wanted to restructure his face.

Mom got up, real fast. "Where have you been?" she asked. "You can't just run off like that."

Before she could hug me, Dad was there, smashing his gut between us. "Go to your room," he said, which was totally laughable. There was no place I'd rather be.

Everybody was screaming. I could hear them from the kitchen, where I checked below the sink for Dad's tackle box. His secret stash. Not exactly a secret. I pulled out a bottle and shoved it in my back pocket.

I slammed the bedroom door, making sure they heard. It didn't matter. They were busy with their own issues. Besides. The High Life was calling. I took out my lighter and hooked it under the bottle cap. Just one twist and it was mine.

The Miller dribbled foam all over the carpet. Great. Now my room stunk like those crackheads on Biscayne Boulevard, the guys with the cardboard signs saying *WILL WORK FOR BEER*. I mopped up the mess with some dirty boxers I'd tossed under the bed. Then I took a long gulp. Dad was yelling in the other room.

"You think this has been a vacation for me?" he said. "Well, it's not Disney World."

Mom was blabbing about "negative emotions" and "talking it out." I could hear everything through the cheap drywall. Yeah, this was officially the worst day in the history of Trent.

I grabbed my iPod and scrolled through the playlists. For some reason, I hadn't deleted my ex's stupid mix. Why? I had no idea. And another mystery I couldn't explain: Why was I listening to it?

Maybe I should've tried harder. Michelle wasn't the perfect girlfriend, but I had no right to judge. And now I was switching schools. This was insane. Part of me was like okay, good. This gives me a chance to start over. I could totally become a different person.

At the same time, I was kind of freaking out. Reality had sunk in. The blank days of Christmas break. Nothing to look forward to in this house. The same empty rhythms. Waste the whole day playing Gears of War on the Xbox. Just me and the Delta Squad.

Man, this sucked.

I chugged the beer so fast, I almost gagged. Soon a fog settled inside me. Usually when I drank alcohol, it turned down the volume in my brain. This time, the beer had the opposite effect. All my dark thoughts multiplied. Their weight dragged me into a black hole, the final resting place for a billion dead suns.

My bedroom door swung open. Dad lurched over to the

desk and sort of collapsed. No respect for privacy whatsoever. He looked so pathetic sitting in that troll-sized chair, gawking at my *Chiefs of America* poster. I couldn't help noticing that he and Sitting Bull had the same pissed-off look.

"Your hair's too long," Dad said.

"Fine. I'll take care of it," I told him. Mom always let it grow when I was a little kid. She said it represented a mighty spirit. If I chopped it off, I'd lose my bond with the universe. How did she know all this stuff? She wasn't Indian.

"And get rid of those headphones," he added. "What're you listening to these days? Hillbilly music?" He grabbed my iPod.

The Miller bottle was on the desk. Bet he could smell the fumes. If you lit a match in my room, it would burst into flames. Too bad this didn't actually happen.

Here's what did happen.

Dad was fumbling with the iPod. He landed on a playlist so old I'd forgotten about it. "What's this? Some bootleg Hendrix?"

I burned with pride. "It's this track I've been working on."

"Want to run that by me again?"

"I wrote it."

The quality was mega shitty. I'd spent a lot of time trying to adjust the recording levels on Audacity, this free software I'd downloaded. Whatever. I could totally do it justice now.

"You know something?" Dad said, wrapping the earbuds around the iPod. No doubt twisting the wires into oblivion. "Son, you don't need that fancy school."

9

The power of music had saved me.

"Your mother's got it in her head," he rambled on. "She's got all these ideas about how things should be."

Wow. He was finally making sense.

"I'm thinking, me and you. Maybe we could live on the Rez."

"The reservation?"

I wasn't exactly jumping with excitement.

The Miccosukee reservation was in the Everglades. The middle of nowhere. I was still getting used to the idea of Dad being around, much less camping with him in some grass-covered chickee hut.

On the other hand, Mom was all kinds of drama. When Dad wasn't around, she was sneaking off with some dude. Mr. Nameless. And she was constantly up in my business. It would only get worse.

"Your mother and I have already discussed it," he said.

"So basically I have no choice?"

Dad eased himself out of the chair. He reached the door and I figured I was home free. Then he looked at the empty beer bottle. I was freaking so bad, waiting for him to explode. He took the Miller and walked into the hall without saying anything. Just closed the door slowly, not making a sound.

The bottle had stamped a ring of dampness in the fake wood. I rubbed my fist through it, but the smear didn't go away.

It probably never would.

My dad is one hundred percent Miccosukee. Ever since

I could remember, I'd heard all these crazy stories about him. Stuff that involved stolen cars, pot brownies, and playing bass in a Jimi Hendrix cover band.

Dad grew up on the Rez. He had to move out once he hooked up with Mom, who is one hundred percent London hippie chick.

That makes me half native, half white, and one hundred percent nothing.

two

The Rez didn't look much different from the flat concrete houses in my old neighborhood. Most houses were painted ice cream colors, lime green and strawberry, all lined up next to a canal laced with water lilies. Each house had its own theme, judging from the life-sized Elvis statue on a front porch. Kids ran around, steering golf carts along the dusty road. I waved to a little girl in a SpongeBob T-shirt. Her bare feet could hardly reach the pedals.

At the end of the block, people docked their airboats. That's how we got to the tree islands in the Everglades. Sometimes this big old gator would swim up to the docks. I'd give him slices of toast and he'd blink, like he was saying thank you.

Me and Dad were staying next door to Uncle Seth in the Little Blue House. More like a shed, it was so damn small. And with Dad around, it was even smaller. The house was behind the Miccosukee Welcome Center. That's where tourists can buy tickets to airboat rides and gator shows.

After we got back home from the cookout, I snuck off with my air rifle. I started blasting a pile of crap my ex-girlfriend gave me. Puka shell necklaces I never wore. A keychain that was supposed to store a hundred digital memories. Instead, it got stuck on one—me and Michelle with our mouths smashed together.

"Which do you like better?" she'd asked, deleting shot after shot.

I'd told her they all looked the same.

Wrong answer.

At first, I tried to set fire to the stuff, but the freaking keychain wouldn't burn. The plastic wrinkled like a slug. So I dumped all that shit on the hood of Dad's Jeep, the "swamp buggy" he left rusting behind the shed. I loaded the rifle and took aim.

The pellets zinged through the trees. I was out there so long, I didn't notice it had started sprinkling. Teensy little drops plinked in my eyes. I blinked them away, squeezed out another round.

The one thing I didn't destroy was her mixtape.

Michelle was a DJ. I mean, she actually spun records instead of just punching buttons on an iPod. She even recorded stuff on cassettes. Michelle made this amazing mix for me over her grandmother's Spoken Rosary on Tape. Between the creeping strings, you could hear nuns chanting like robots.

Her parents weren't too thrilled once I started hanging around. I'd pull up in the monster-sized Jeep, which I called

"The Yeti." Then one of her frathead cousins would materialize on the front lawn. I couldn't even keep their names straight.

"So how about them Marlins?" Brian (or Ryan?) would mumble.

Baseball was never my thing. Maybe if Dad had been around, he could've taught me the basics.

I must've been brain-dead not to realize Michelle was playing me. A couple weeks before I moved out to the Rez, we were making out in my room and her stupid cell kept buzzing against my leg. She just shrugged and tossed the phone in her purse. Later, she got up to use the bathroom and I checked her text messages. Yeah, it was shady thing to do. Not half as shady as what I saw:

Eric: I can't wait to see u babe.

I scrolled through the list of callers. Michelle knew so many people at school, it was hard to keep track. She would clomp through the hall shrieking some freshman girl's name, then swoop her into a bone-crushing hug as if they were going off to war. It was kind of annoying.

When I asked about the message, she got mad, of course.

"Don't you trust me?" Michelle chewed her lower lip. Her teeth were a little crooked. She'd been lazy about wearing her retainer, but I didn't care. I buried my face in her neck, breathed in the burnt popcorn smell of that gunk she used to "sculpt" her split ends.

I wanted to tell her that I didn't trust anybody.

———————

When I got home after school, Dad was slumped in a beach chair behind the Little Blue House like he'd just woken up from a nap. There was no escaping him.

"Target practice, huh?" he said, looking at the mess.

"Something like that."

"We should go down to Trail Glades. Shoot some skeet," he said as we headed into the house.

Now he was making scissors with his meaty fingers, pretending to snip my hair. For a guy who'd been eating off prison cafeteria trays, he looked more like a Mexican wrestler than a menace to society.

He was already making plans for the weekend. "Is that bowling place still open? You know. The one near Dolphin Mall?"

"I think it got torn down," I said, which wasn't true.

"Really? That's a shame."

A twinge of guilt shot through me. "Maybe it's still there. Whatever. It was kind of ghetto. I'll look into it."

A promise I wouldn't keep.

Dad tapped my arm. "Where's that bowling bag you used to carry everywhere? The one with the robots?"

The last time I'd gone bowling, I was in fourth grade. It was somebody's birthday. Luke Swisstack. Why was I even there? I couldn't stand that kid. He used to make fun of me nonstop. He'd point at the toilets in the boy's bathroom, the lids stamped with the word *TRENTON* in loopy capital letters.

"Hey Trent," he'd say, laughing like crazy. "Is this what you're named after?"

My cell was ringing. Shouting, actually. The voice of Drake, rapping about how he wanted it to be "forever."

I glanced at the screen.

Michelle.

"Do these things really take pictures?" Dad swooped over and grabbed the phone. Snatched it right out of my hand. He held it up to the light, as if he could see inside it.

"Yeah," I said, snatching it back. "And you can make movies and stuff."

"Could you show me?"

"Sure. No problem."

"I mean, when you've got time."

"Okay, Dad." I inched toward the door.

He grinned. "Time is one thing we've got plenty of."

Dad had been out of jail since December, but after we moved to the Rez, it seemed he was suddenly everywhere. I'd come home from school and he'd be passed out on the couch. Lights off. TV blasting. He'd reach for the remote, put the Travel Channel on mute. Then the questions would start rolling.

Like they were now.

"How're you liking that new school?" he asked.

"Fine."

Christmas break had just ended. Nobody was liking school. Including me. Mom wasn't happy about me going to Palm Hammock, but Dad said it was good enough. I had to wake up at the buttcrack of dawn and take the Florida Turnpike. My old neighborhood was a long haul from the Everglades. Almost an hour.

"Maybe you could try the school on the Rez?" Dad suggested.

Hell no. I was spending enough time there. Uncle Seth already had me working at the Miccosukee Indian Village on weekends, collecting tips for the gator show.

"Better work on those grades," Dad told me. "Because if you screw up, there's no second chances. Understand?"

He never gave a flying rip about my grades before. Now it was too late. Did he really think he could just act like things were normal?

"And no girls," he added. "You need to keep your head straight."

I was trying so hard not to laugh. Who was he kidding? No girls? Like that was going to happen. And I had my own questions. Lots of them. I still didn't understand why he got busted. I was a little kid when Dad "went away." Mom filled me in on the minor details. Nothing dramatic like first-degree murder. He got caught writing bad checks. That's all. To be totally honest, I almost wished he'd robbed a bank.

After these non-conversations, I'd sneak off to my room

and plug Rock Band into the Xbox. Seconds later, Dad would appear behind me, hovering like the Nazgûl from *Lord of the Rings*. It was majorly weird, the way he drifted around the Little Blue House.

"What you need is a real instrument, not a toy," he'd tell me. "Soon as I get some cash, I'll buy you a real nice bass. A Hagstrom 8-string."

Right.

My Uncle Seth was supposed to help Dad in the job department. Something he couldn't possibly screw up. So far, I wasn't holding my breath. Dad mowed lawns and washed cars. When we lived at Mom's place, he'd polished the kitchen table so many times I could scrape my initials into the wax.

We had a routine. It was called do-as-you-wish. We ate dinner whenever we felt like it, usually Lean Cuisine lasagna in front of CNN. But tonight, Dad set out place mats and our stupid Tiki Man salt shakers. He insisted we hold hands while he muttered a prayer:

Heavenly Father, we are grateful for the food we are about to receive... blah blah... nourishment of our bodies... blah blah... Amen.

I closed my eyes and beamed myself to another dimension.

When I scraped back my chair, Dad frowned.

"Going somewhere?"

"Out." I zipped myself into my sweatshirt, tugged up the hood.

He wasn't buying it. "Listen up, kiddo," he said, like I was ten years old, the exact age he'd bailed on me. "It's Tuesday. You got school tomorrow."

"No shit."

"Watch your mouth. I don't want to hear that kind of language in this house."

What's the big freaking deal? Dad was sweating like a preacher on one of those Jesus channels, going on about bad habits and taking the high road. Did he really expect me to buy this crap?

I scooped my keys off the counter. "My boy Alvaro's spinning at the Vagabond."

Alvaro lived behind a golf course in Coral Gables. He had his own "music studio" in the garage. He also had a grandma who paid for it. We always talked about starting a band. Of course, this never happened. When I got kicked out of Southwinds, Alvaro thought it was hilarious. Maybe that's why I'd been avoiding his calls. I really didn't feel like explaining my life situation to him. Don't get me wrong, Alvaro was cool. But I kind of doubted that he understood.

"You're not leaving this house," Dad said.

"I promised I'd go. You know. Moral support."

It's sad to admit this…but I couldn't help wondering if Michelle would be there. We were officially over, but she hadn't stopped texting me. I refused to acknowledge her existence ever since I'd read that sketchy text on her phone. (Okay, I was snooping. Trust me. I had my reasons.) The girl flat-out cheated. Then she had the balls to lie about it. That's so messed up.

19

Anyway.

Dad smacked the keys out of my hand. They clattered across the linoleum, spun, and landed in a heap a few feet away from the table. Both of us stared at that spot, daring the other to move first. Instead, I grabbed my skateboard and escaped out the front door.

I skated to the docks, watched the men haul their boats from the water. At this point I was freaked, thanks to Dad yelling at me. I bummed a cigarette off this guy who kept dragging his boat onto the concrete, only to let it roll backward with a splash.

Talk about random. I'm no fan of cancer sticks, thank you very much. I just held the smoke in my mouth. After a couple puffs, I flicked it away. The waves were shiny with rainbow-colored bubbles. In the distance, a line of trailers clattered down the road, tugging their dripping boats behind them.

Later that night I was online, watching people act idiotic on ChatRandom. This emo-looking girl kept shaking a raccoon puppet at the camera. After a few desperate attempts at a conversation that didn't involve sign language or stuffed animals, I was about to sign off when Michelle sent me a DM.

Michy1996: hey sexy. i miss you <3

I blinked at the screen. No explanation. Not even a simple "I'm sorry." What the hell was she thinking? I stared until the words morphed into hieroglyphics. Then I sent a reply:

T-Rex: You left a bunch of crap with me

I didn't mention that most of it was (a) burned beyond recognition, (b) riddled with bb pellets, (c) all the above.

Michy1996: maybe i can come over???

T-REX: if you feel like driving 20 miles
to the Everglades

I waited for her to go away.

Michy1996: text me the address? :)

Man, that girl had balls. I'd give her that much. I wanted to tell her that I stayed awake at night listening to her playlist; that I still found her curly hair all over my clothes; that she was the first girl.

The first everything.

———

Michelle parked her car on the front lawn, which Dad had just mowed. I didn't want to deal with him, so we snuck through the yard and headed straight for my room.

"So this is your new place. Are you going to give me a tour?" Michelle stretched out on my "bed," an old sleeping bag I'd unrolled on the floor. I always thought she looked good without any makeup. Her damp curls were scraped into a ponytail. God, she was hot.

"Okay. Let's do this like *MTV Cribs*. There's my amazing walk-in closet," I said, pointing at a heap of rumpled T-shirts. "And that's the entertainment center." I kicked my headphones out of the way.

"Very nice, Trenton. I really like your toys," she said, glancing at the army of Orc Shamans lined up on a shelf. For the record, I never played D&D. I just collected the miniatures. When I got stressed, I used to chew on their shields. It's unimaginable that I didn't get lead poisoning.

"What else do you like?" I asked, stroking her arm.

Michelle slipped her hands under my T-shirt. She let her fingers slide down, ever so slowly, and whispered, "This."

I stared at her pale, unlipsticked mouth and waited for the lies to start rolling. Instead, she kissed me. Hard.

I didn't plan on having sex. It just sort of happened.

We didn't talk much afterwards. I listened to a dog yapping down the block. Sometimes he got so freaked out, it sounded like hiccups. Why did they get a dog if they were just going to leave it outside?

Later, we snuck out to Michelle's car and drove off. I wasn't sure if Dad noticed, but I wasn't sticking around to find out.

I cranked the radio, scanned around until we landed on a pirate station—one of those illegal deals, hidden in a haze of static. The DJ played an entire Tupac record, dirty words and all. When people called to complain, he hung up on them.

Michelle giggled as I tried to mimic his voice, rolling my R's like crazy. Everything was cool again.

"Please don't hate me," she said. "I've known Eric forever. He's like my little brother. For real. I'm the one who should be pissed. Why were you going through my phone? I always feel like you're judging me."

That's how evil Michelle could be. She twisted things so basically I was the one thinking I'd done wrong. How dense is that? I was on the verge of apologizing when my cell rang. I glanced at the number.

"Shit," I muttered.

Michelle cupped her long fingers on my knee. "Who's that?"

"Nobody. Just Dad."

She smirked. "Are you in trouble?"

"I was supposed to do something. No big deal."

We slowed for a red light. Michelle leaned in closer.

"Can it wait?" she whispered.

Yeah. It could wait.

As we kissed, I was barely aware of the car horns blasting behind us. The light changed and still, I couldn't pull my mouth from hers. It was like nothing else existed: only her lips, their softness, and the warmth of her tongue sliding over mine.

After the epic makeout session, we drove to this triple-decker mall off the highway. Michelle wanted to go to One-Up. Or to be more specific, the bar at One-Up.

"They're kind of whatever about checking I.D.s there," Michelle said, slipping her pinkie inside the waistband of my Levis. Damn. That girl could've asked me to backstroke, butt-naked and blindfolded, across the Everglades, and I would've said *yes, please, thank you.*

One-Up was in complete chaos when we pushed through the double doors. Kids stomped their sneakered feet in time to *Dance Dance Revolution.* Underaged thugs were pelting nachos at a girl in line for "virtual bowling." I thought about Dad and the promise I'd made to hang with him.

"I'm not really into places that use tickets as a form of currency," I said.

Michelle stuck out her lower lip. "You're not pussying out on me?"

"Hell no." I glanced at the neon-splattered bar. It reminded me of a UFO. At least the way UFOs look in Hollywood movies: a fortress of blinking lights. I edged closer, plopped myself onto a stool.

The bartender lifted his goateed face at me.

"This is a joke, right?" He squeezed a wedge of lime into somebody's overpriced beer.

"No worries," I said, ripping open my stupid Velcro wallet. "I got I.D."

He squinted at the driver's license, the one courtesy of my boy, Alvaro, and his Heat Seal lamination machine.

"Listen, *Joe Consuelo*," the bartender said, flicking it back. "If you don't drag your skinny ass out of here, I'm calling the cops."

Meanwhile, Michelle was making smoochy faces at me. I shook my head no. Party's over.

"What happened?" she asked, as I ducked in front of a widescreen projection of NASCAR Sprint Cup racing.

"Nothing happened," I said, yanking her towards the exit.

We sat on the steps outside, next to a fish-shaped fountain that reeked of bleach. The grates were clogged with pennies. Did people really believe their wishes would come true if they threw change away? I was half-tempted to scoop out a handful, but it seemed like bad karma.

"We should get going." I tried to stroke Michelle's hair, but she turned her whole body away from me. All she cared about was that stupid bar. It was like I didn't exist.

"Oh, my god. There's Jess," said Michelle, pointing at a group of people from my old school. "Don't you think she looks pretty?"

There was no correct answer to this question.

Michelle ran over to them, clopping in her heels. She left me there on the steps, along with her purse and cell phone. As usual, it was buzzing with text messages. I picked it up and the first thing I saw was that dude's name.

She'd played me once.

I wasn't going to be played again.

I got up and started walking to the mall exit. How was I going to get home? Here's a better question: Why the hell did I care? I wasn't going straight back to the Rez. Not right now. Maybe I could bum a ride off Alvaro. He was always down for beer, which is exactly what I needed.

"Where are you going?" Michelle shouted at me.

"Away from you."

I kept my mouth shut. No more talking. At that point, I was done. Really done.

I walked across the street to the Metrorail. When the train finally whooshed into the station, I got on and stared out the window. All the glass panels were blurred with scratchy tags. Through the swollen letters, I watched the traffic stream ahead, start and stop again. Then the train lurched forward, carrying me above the streetlights.

three

In homeroom, I passed out on my desk. I could still taste the beers from last night. Guess I was a little hungover. The space between my eyebrows was pounding like a quadruple drum solo. Even the smallest noise made it throb harder. Nothing a few energy drinks couldn't fix.

The morning announcements crackled at an obtuse angle above my head. After an endless stream of Career Fair updates and dress code violations, I finally drifted back to consciousness. In my sleep-deprived state, I barely noticed the girl with the purple-streaked hair reading the lunch specials on the TV.

Pippa McCormick goes to this school?

This girl used to be my best friend. I called her Pippa-Down-The-Street because she lived in my old neighborhood. That was a long time ago, back when we were kids. Pippa didn't look like a kid anymore. In fact, she looked amazing.

The guys behind me were mooing like brain-dead cows.

Their complete lack of maturity was damn pitiful. It really got me bent. I mean, come on. What was this? Kindergarten?

When Pippa read the principal's hit list (aka the "Walk of Shame"), I snapped awake. I must've been in a coma or something. For a minute I'd thought she called my name.

"Could...um...Trent Osceola see the principal in his office?" Even Pippa sounded confused. The words replayed in my head.

Could I see the principal?

Sure.

Would I?

Not a chance in hell.

Mrs. Kemp shooed me out the door. Free at last. I made a beeline for the library, my hiding place. As I pounded downstairs, I almost slammed into the guidance counselor, a middle-aged dude with a Looney Tunes tie, Velcro sneakers, and a name I couldn't remember. He always pretended like he was on your side, but I wasn't falling for it.

"Hey kiddo. We need to chat," Mr. Velcro said, breathing nicotine fumes all over me. The man had no concept of personal space. He stuck out his hand. Obviously, I was supposed to shake it.

Too bad I've never been a fan of handshakes.

Mr. Velcro dropped his arm to his side. "Guess you got the call."

"What call?" I glared at his stupid tie: Wile. E. Coyote waving goodbye as he cartwheeled off a cliff. I always felt sorry for him, not that freaking smartass, Road Runner.

"You've just transferred to this school, Trent, and we're already hearing reports of you missing class." Mr. Velcro stroked his wedding band. I tried to imagine who would pledge eternal love to this freak. Maybe someone even freakier.

"Who's 'we'?"

"Believe me. I've got a kid in braces, but I was young once." He laughed. When I didn't, he kept blabbing. "So we discussed it and we're thinking, what the heck? Let's give you a chance. Hear your side of the story. We feel that's the right thing to do, in this particular case."

We, we, we.

God, who talks like that? The Queen of France?

Mr. Velcro steered me into the principal's office. The walls were covered with laminated posters. Sunsets melting into the beach. Kittens dangling off a window. Feel-good slogans with the empty enthusiasm of a pep rally: *Teamwork. Many hands. One goal.*

Above the principal's chair, a crashing wave urged me to *adjust my attitude* because it's a *powerful force.* You could say the same about hurricanes.

"Have a seat, Mr … Oss … " The principal squinted at a paper on his desk. No doubt the legendary "permanent record."

Sound it out. Ah-See-Oh-La.

He was staring at my trapper hat. Yeah, it doesn't exactly fit South Florida, but it keeps me warm when old lady teachers crank the AC.

"Trent, could you remove your hat, please?"

I could, but ...

He took out a hankie and wiped his glasses. "Do you know why you're here?"

It sounded like a philosophical question. Why *was* I here?

He waited.

I tugged off my hat and plopped it on my knee. "Well, they called my name on the announcements ..." I trailed off, thinking of Pippa, her sweet voice.

"True. This is true." He glanced at Mr. Velcro, who sat next to me, jiggling his sneaker like a bass pedal. "We've been going over your records ..."

Again with the "we."

" ... and it seems we've detected a pattern."

I sunk a little lower in my chair.

"Your attendance is spotty and you haven't been here long. You transferred to Palm Hammock with poor grades. Until last year, it looks like you were doing well. Is something going on at home? Maybe you'd like to talk about it?"

No thanks.

"Help us out, Trent." Mr. Velcro woke up. "What's in your head? Could you share with us?"

I shrugged. "I'm not big on sharing."

At Southwinds, I passed every test without studying. All I had to do was listen. I didn't even write stuff down or take notes or anything. I just paid attention. That's the secret. But I flaked out on my homework. That's what killed my grades. It's so damn stupid. Why did I have to fill out a worksheet on Reading Comprehension if I already knew all the answers?

I could've asked Mr. Velcro the same thing. Instead, I said, "They put me in all these baby classes."

The principal drummed his fat fingers on the desk. "Is that why you haven't been attending?"

"I missed homeroom yesterday. That's because my car died and I live all the way out in the Everglades and my dad won't get it fixed."

"You're living where?" The principal took off his glasses, as if that would help him hear better.

Shit.

"I was at my dad's house." Not exactly a lie.

"So, your family situation ... "

"What about it?"

He wouldn't let up. "You mentioned your father. Our records show that you live with your mother in Kendall."

"I'm not talking about my dad, okay? Just leave him out of it."

The principal slid open a drawer and grabbed a pen. He scribbled something on his mountain of papers. "At this rate, you're in danger of repeating your junior year."

The word "danger" made me flinch. Believe me. If I dropped out of school, I wasn't coming back. No reset button. No second chances. Isn't that what Dad said?

"You've still got time," Mr. Velcro added. "If you really push through this semester ... "

Blah, blah, blah.

I watched his gums flap while I hit the mute button inside my head. Sometimes I make up songs—riffs or lyrical refrains—when people talk at me. At least I put those seconds to good use. It wasn't like I was missing anything while they pretended to care about my "lack of family structure."

Here's a newsflash. Nobody really cares.

When he finally shut up, I tuned the volume back on.

"Any questions?" Mr. Velcro tapped his foot.

"Yeah," I said, hopping out of my chair. The hat flopped across the floor like a tumbleweed. I plunked it onto my head. "Can I go now?"

On the way out, I passed the dust-encrusted TV in the front office. Then I saw Pippa on the TV again and my brain went into some kind of nuclear meltdown. It was more like a stream-of-consciousness, like we talked about in AP English.

"What class is that?" I jabbed my thumb at the TV.

The secretary didn't even look at me. "Digital Filmmaking and Communications."

It sounded easy enough.

"Sign me up," I said.

"You'll have to ask Mr. Bonette for permission," she said. "The class is very popular. It might already be filled."

I didn't even ask for a late pass. Just stumbled out the door and headed for the stairs.

"Wait." The secretary was actually following me like a creeper. "Where do you think you're going?"

What a dumb-ass question. I was going to the film class. Or, to be more specific, the TV studio. Walking real careful through the hall. Quietly. Almost Zenlike.

The secretary didn't look very Zen. I wanted to explain the concept to her, but she was fired up about my hat.

"Not allowed on school grounds..." She was spitting all over me, which was beyond gross. Let's just say I wasn't listening.

I took a step backward, as if pulled by gravitational forces toward the men's room. The secretary didn't let up. I half-expected her to follow me in there.

"I'm giving you a warning," she said.

That's the part where I was supposed to act all grateful. "Thanks," I muttered as the door banged shut. Thanks for nothing.

I leaned against the tiled walls. Recently, I'd spent a lot of time looking for places to hide during class. Sometimes I walked over to the elementary school library. (Not that I'm a pervert or whatever. They had these nice beanbag chairs. I'd sink into my own little corner and read graphic novels.) True, I could've finished my junior year on the Rez, but technically my address was still in Kendall. I never thought I'd get stuck in regular school again. Not that Palm Hammock seemed much different than Southwinds. The teachers made you memorize a bunch of pointless facts. Why didn't they teach something useful, like how to get a refund on your taxes?

To be totally honest, I figured the film class was an easy A. I couldn't afford to fail another semester. After watching the morning announcements, my comatose brain put two and two together. That's when I had an epiphany (my new favorite vocab word):

Pippa could help me.

I hid in the bathroom, trying to think of how to approach her. I could walk up, all casual, like *Hey, didn't we used to play pirates?*

The more I thought about it, the dumber it sounded. I could always just bump into her during class and let her do all the talking. That was the cowardly way out. But it's hard to feel brave when you're splashing your face in a graffiti-stained sink, hunched under a dozen felt-tip penis doodles.

As I dipped back into the hallway, I was still juggling opening lines, testing them out like bass guitar riffs. I was so busy concentrating, I didn't notice Kenzie Shoemaker marching straight toward me. She had a bitchy look on her face and a cell phone in her hand. A bad combo.

"I just heard what you did to Michelle," she told me.

Nice. I'd escaped from one school only to find that Michelle had a posse here too. Sort of like a female mafia. I really wasn't in the mood to deal with it. I stared at the little blond hairs sparkling above her lip while she gave me the third degree.

"She deserves so much better," Kenzie said. "Why did you leave her last night?"

Now I was pissed. "First of all, Michelle played me. Not the other way around."

"Obviously, this proves what she said about you." Kenzie stood there, waiting for me to ask the inevitable question.

"Okay. I give up. What did Michelle say?"

"You're not good enough for her."

This hurt on so many levels. Did Michelle really say that? I mean, did she really think I wasn't good enough?

I shoved past Kenzie and crashed into the water fountain. For some reason, it was always clogged. Water dribbled over the edge and splattered all over me. I stared at a wad of gum plopped like a stalagmite near the drain. (Or was it stalactite? I always got them confused.)

"That was slick," said Kenzie, walking away.

My jeans were covered with damp splotches. No way could I talk to Pippa now. I opened my locker and pretended to look for something. What if Pippa walked by? I waited a couple minutes, hoping she'd materialize. Then I saw Kenzie clomping down the hall again. In my mind, I heard the Imperial Death March from *Star Wars*.

I'd had enough of Kenzie's bullshit, so I walked back toward the auditorium. I couldn't stand having my life broadcast all over this school. Michelle didn't even go here. It was beyond embarrassing. Not to mention totally unfair.

The double doors clanked as I slammed my weight into them. All the chairs in the auditorium were folded near the stage, making the walls look bigger than usual. I was kind of nervous about barging into the TV studio, but that's exactly what I did.

Heads turned as I marched into the brightly lit room. Already I felt like I'd made a big mistake. The people in this class were probably film geniuses and I was an expert at nothing. In the back was a camera on a tripod, along with lots of bell-shaped lamps, a semicircle of desks, and Pippa.

She was looking at me. I mean, really looking. I could practically feel it—the stare of epic proportions, like Storm in the X-Men, igniting the classroom into an Apocalypse-worthy solar flare.

Damn.

When we were little, Pippa McCormick got mistaken for a boy on a daily basis. I seriously doubted that she had that problem anymore. For one thing, her purple-streaked hair spilled all the way down to her butt. I didn't know girls could grow it that long. Guess I figured they came with an "off" switch when it reached a certain length, like, say, their shoulder blades or whatever.

The teacher was sitting on his desk. He was kind of young-ish and thin, but not in an anorexic sort of way.

"Are you looking for Digital Filmmaking and Communications?" he asked. "This class is full. I shouldn't let anybody else in."

"Really? Because I'm pretty good at communicating."

I waited for him to get pissed. Instead, he just smirked. "I'm Mr. Bonette. Call me Mr. Bones if you like."

Okay. This teacher was definitely not normal.

Mr. Bones reached into a drawer and took out a folder. "I didn't catch your name."

"It's Trent." God, this was so awkward.

"Have you taken any film classes before?" he wanted to know.

"No, but I've watched a lot of movies."

The girls in the front row laughed. Yeah, I sounded like a complete idiot.

He wrote something in his folder. "What kind of movies?"

At this point, my mind went blank. "Um. I don't know. Documentaries. Real-life stuff." I figured this would get him off my case.

"Excellent. You're into *cinéma vérité*."

So now we were in French class. "Cinema what?"

"It means truth-film."

The front-row girls were laughing again. They almost fell out of their chairs. Actually, that would be pretty funny.

"Do you want to be here, Trent?" he asked.

What was I supposed to say? No, I don't want to be here at school, talking to a teacher who thinks I'm stupid. I don't want to be home, either. Wherever that is. Stuck in the Everglades. It didn't matter where I went, because nobody cared.

Mr. Bones waited. "Okay, I'll fit you in. If you want to stay here, grab a chair. We're about to go over the rule of thirds."

Rule of what? I thought we were going to watch movies.

This class was looking to be a lot harder than I'd thought.

While Mr. Bones rambled on about framing the subject, I was busy checking out Pippa's checkered legs. She kept them bouncing at all times, as if listening to a never-ending soundtrack inside her head.

Pippa used to wear jeans, like, every single day. Now her slamming body was packed into checkered tights and a dress that looked safety-pinned together. Upon closer inspection, I realized the safety pins were staples.

This was the girl who'd played mad scientist with me. We'd raid the fridge, dump chocolate syrup and mayo in a cup, and dare each other to chug it. We used to talk about all kinds of stuff. Then I got into Southwinds in middle school and we kind of stopped talking. I'm not even sure why.

Did she remember me?

The bell rang and everybody jumped like a bunch of dogs. "Listen up, people," Mr. Bones yelled. "Before you leave, let's talk about your final project for this semester. It's a group project."

Now I had to do a group project? I'd thought this was supposed to be an easy class. My life depended on it. God, this was going to suck so bad.

"Where's my documentary fan?" He waved at me. Yeah, just pile on the humiliation. "I need you guys to team up in pairs. You're going to work together and film Life Portraits—documentaries of each other's family life."

A groan washed over the classroom.

"What if my family life is boring?" I asked.

"Your partner's job is to make it not boring," he said. "There will be a screening of your films at the end of the semester, in the auditorium."

Great.

"No 'talking head' interviews like you see on TV," he went on. "You must use the vocabulary of shots that we've discussed in class. Wide Angle, Close up, Reverse..."

"All of them?"

Mr. Bones stared. That's the problem with teachers. They aren't fluent in sarcasm.

"Yes, all of them," he said. "But not at the same time."

Okay. Maybe I was wrong.

Pippa was the first to grab the sign-up sheet. I got stuck in line behind the front-row girls. They kept arguing about switching partners. It was totally annoying. When I grabbed the sign-up sheet, there were no spaces left.

My eyes moved across the page. At the top was Pippa's signature in capital letters, and next to it, she'd written my name.

four

As I pushed my way back through the auditorium, a bunch of theater girls shoved themselves in front of me. For some unknown reason, they were carrying one of the legless CPR dummies from health class. Even worse: they were singing "Happy Birthday" to it.

Pippa was sitting alone on the stage. I headed for the stairs and tripped halfway up. (Who's dumb enough to fall *up* stairs? That's how uncoordinated I am.) Meanwhile, the theater girls were laughing like a public service announcement: *We're having more fun than you.*

"Oh, my god, Trent," Pippa said. "This is crazy. I was reading the morning announcements and when I saw your name, I was like, whoa. Since when do you go to Palm Hammock?"

Maybe I could've said something about her purple-streaked hair. It looked so amazing, like a punk rock fairy queen. I could've mentioned the way she strutted in those crazy boots, so tall and straight, while the other girls slouched around looking insecure. I could've asked if she still believed in monsters like the Wendigo.

I could've said a lot of things.

What did I say?

"I got sent to the principal's office."

"For what? A dress code violation?" she asked.

"Nah. I usually just come to school naked."

Why the hell did I say that? Once somebody mentions the word "naked," it's kind of impossible to hit the ignore button in your head. Now I was imagining my former BFF in the buff. The mental picture was beyond my control.

"That's probably not going to win you any fans," she told me.

"Don't be a hater." I leaned in close and whispered, "My fans are legion."

"Excuse me, Mr. Popular. I didn't know you had fans."

"Well, there's a lot you don't know. About me, I mean." I hooked my thumb around Pippa's.

One, two, three, four. I declare a thumb war.

"Are you kidding?" she said. "I know all your dirty secrets."

"Yeah, well. Now I've got new ones. Even secreter secrets. And dirtier, too."

God, that didn't come out right.

I pointed at the avalanche of papers on the stage next to her. "Is this for class?" On each page was a box with stick people floating inside it. Next to the boxes, she'd written things like *Close-up of zombie teeth.*

"They're storyboards," she said. "I make lots of drawings so I can tell what my movie is going to look like. This is my zombie screenplay. It's going to be epic...if I can actually finish it. I have no idea what we should do for our final project."

"Me neither. But I can't fail this class."

"This is so weird. I mean, the last time we had class together was Mrs. Campbell's social studies, in sixth grade."

"I know, right? My brain is exploding right now." I grabbed one of her Sharpies and drew a pentagram on the toe of my sneaker.

Pippa was trying to sling an enormous camera bag over her shoulder. "I hate carrying all this stuff around. But it's my baby, you know?"

"I'll carry it for you," I said, stepping on her foot. Luckily, she was wearing these heavy-duty combat boots. "Hey, do you think I could get a good grade in this class? Or is it like...for experts?"

"I'm no expert. Believe me," she said, holding the door.

I winced in the burst of sunlight. "You think I could pass?"

"Have you actually shot a film before?" she asked.

"Um. No," I said.

"I used to make little stop-motion films with my grandpa's old-school Bolex. That camera is practically indestructible. People strapped them on planes during World War II and recorded the bombs as they dropped."

I kept thinking how it felt so easy, talking to Pippa. It was like we'd never stopping talking. Everybody was running to their next class, making so much noise I could barely hear myself think. I wanted to hit the mute button on the world.

"Aren't you supposed to be studying music?" she asked. "I mean, you got into that special school and everything."

I flinched. "It's not that special."

When she said "special," it sounded like a school for people with mental problems. Then again, I had problems she didn't know about.

I took out the Sharpie and wrote a string of digits on her hand. "I'm at my dad's place now. This is the number, in case you want to talk about film stuff. Is your phone the same?"

"You probably don't even remember it."

"Hell yes I do."

"Prove it."

I recited the numbers. Perfectly.

"Wow, Trent. That was kind of impressive. I better give you my cell. Don't call the house, okay? My mom's been kind of weird lately."

"Yeah? She used to be so cool."

"My mom?"

"Yeah. What's wrong with Mama Dukes?" I asked.

Pippa looked away. "She's just…"

"It's cool. Didn't mean to get up in your business." I stuck out my arm for her number.

The Sharpie kept dying, so she pressed extra hard. "Sorry," she said, as if it were her fault. "This pen is untrustworthy."

I scanned the hallway. "What are you going to do now?"

"Go to my next class, I guess. God, that sounds lame."

"Sure you don't want to go exploring?" I asked, walking backward toward the auditorium doors.

"Maybe next time. There's a quiz on Technology of the Future that I'm destined to fail."

"In the future, you mean?"

She laughed. "Something like that."

"Okay. Catch you later." I lunged down the sidewalk, probably scaring everyone trying to get stoned in the parking lot.

I didn't feel like going to class. Not after my amazing conversation with Pippa. School was almost tolerable once everybody headed back to their pre-assigned rooms like good little robots. I spent the rest of the afternoon power-napping in the Yeti. I kept the windows rolled down so I didn't suffocate to death. That is, until I was rudely awakened.

"What's the problem here?"

A face—sunburned and buzzcut—hovered above me. The campus security dude was talking about the dangers of sleeping in a car. Obviously, this was the most exciting moment of his entire week.

"Dentist appointment," I muttered. I almost ran the guy over, backing out of the lot. Not that it would've been a total tragedy.

The security dude was mega pissed now, scribbling on his memo pad (my license plate, no doubt). He circled the lot in his creaky little golf cart. What a freaking joke. How was he supposed to protect us from terrorists? He didn't even carry a gun.

Nothing to do now except drive back to the Rez. It took forever to get there from school. My dad was probably hanging around the house, like usual. Just thinking about him made my stomach burn. Then I realized I'd had nothing to eat all day, not counting the Gummi Bears that I'd "borrowed" from some random girl this morning. She only gave me the yellow ones.

As I contemplated my fast food options (McRib is back!), my cell phone buzzed inside the glove box. I slowed for a red light, then reached over and dug it out.

Yo. I usually don't do mass mailings like this
but... I've been working on some sick new beats.
If you haven't downloaded my tracks online,
you've been sleeping hard...

Nothing like a mass mailing (in this case, for Michelle's lame-ass DJ set at Churchill's on Sunday) to make you feel special. Why did she bother inviting me—along with three hundred of her closest friends? We weren't friends. So what did that make us?

I needed to find out.

———

The Rez was home. Too bad it didn't feel like it.

When I'd left Mom's house, I didn't expect to miss things like clean laundry and a regular feeding schedule. I just wanted to get away from her. Now I was starting to regret it.

Sometimes I wanted to jump in an airboat and take off (as far as possible).

A couple days after I moved out here, I was watching the boats out on the water. Dad said it was for a funeral. He didn't go into much explanation.

"What happens next?" I asked him.

He shrugged. "Your body goes back to the earth."

"And then what? Do you believe in heaven and all that?"

"You move on to the spirit world."

"Even if you do bad stuff?"

"We move on. The animals move on. That's the way it goes."

So I guess Dad didn't believe in hell.

One time back in Kendall, I stayed awake all night, playing the Xbox. I was so freaking exhausted I basically passed out. I would've stayed in that semi-comatose state, but Dad woke me up. He said it was dangerous, falling asleep at dusk. Your spirit might leave your body and never return.

"Bullshit." I'd tugged the blanket over my head, but couldn't fall back to sleep.

Today, Dad was the one in danger of losing his spirit. He was conked out, facedown on the floor as if he'd tried to do a push-up and just stayed that way. I shook him hard, and he finally snapped to life. The whole situation made me feel awkward. I started blabbing about school, the film I was going to make. Dad was all into it.

"Let's do some movies," he said.

I brought out the video camera I'd borrowed from class.

Dad was posing like the Hulk, which was pretty hilarious. I took a few practice shots, but honestly, I had no idea what I was doing.

"Mr. Hollywood," he said. "I was in a movie once."

He showed me an envelope stuffed with black-and-white publicity stills. It was for a documentary about life in the Everglades. He gave me the whole speech about his rock band, how they'd played a special show just for the film crew. The footage was never used. The director only wanted traditional shots of the Miccosukees—elder ladies stringing beads, kids paddling a kayak, bare-chested men hacking through the swamp with machetes. That kind of shit.

"What happened to the concert footage?" I asked.

Dad shoved the pictures in the envelope. "Gone."

"Ever think about getting the band together? That would be awesome."

He was looking at a crack in the wall, toward the west, the land of the dead. "Son, there's nobody left."

I didn't get it. "Then maybe I could play bass with you?"

"Maybe," he said.

———

I made the drive on Sunday and hung around outside Churchill's, but Michelle was late as usual. No point waiting for her sorry ass any longer. I fumbled for the blunt rolled in my sock, sparked up behind the double-decker bus (it's always parked in the same place, facing Second Avenue). Checked the time for the umpteenth time: 11:11 p.m. Make a wish.

One of the DJs had already dragged their gear into the street—portable amps and snakelike cables, milk crates stuffed with old-school records: *Thrilling Chilling Sounds in Stereo*, *The Song of the Humpback Whale*.

"Hey, Trenton."

Nobody called me that anymore. Unless it was she-who-shall-remain-nameless.

My ex was all skanked out in her DJ getup: silver gladiator sandals laced to the knee, a stretchy tube top that reminded me of tinfoil. In other words, hot in a desperate sort of way. But I refused to think of Michelle in that category anymore. Or any category.

"I like your style," Michelle said. "Seriously. I'm feeling the wilderness effect. What's that thing on your head?"

"A trapper hat," I mumbled.

"And what are you trapping in downtown Miami?"

Her backup crew laughed like this was the funniest joke ever. Of course, things are always funny when you're wasted.

Here's what I wanted to say:

1. You suck.

2. Thanks for destroying my life. Why did I waste my entire Christmas break trying to make sense of this fucked-up relationship?

3. I just pretended to like all those fake-ass bands on your stupid mixtape. I mean, come on. Who's dumb enough to attempt a techno mashup of the *Braveheart* soundtrack? That shit is classic.

Of course, I didn't say any of this.

"Hey." Michelle plucked the blunt from my fingers. "How's it going?"

How's it going? How did she think it's going?

"Do you want your mix back?" I asked.

"My what?" She sucked in a mouthful of smoke.

"You know. The mixtape you made for me."

"Mixtape?"

Silence.

"You can keep it." Michelle coughed.

There was nothing else to say.

I filled the emptiness with something idiotic. "It's just that … you worked so hard on it. I mean, it's really tight."

"I just sort of threw it together," Michelle was saying.

This was the girl who told me about exploding stars, how everything on Earth is made from their death—even the iron in our blood. Meanwhile, her groupies were passing around my blunt.

"I enjoyed the idea of playing bass guitar … more than actually playing it," this dude was saying. He watched me watching them.

"Just trying to figure out where you're going with this silent treatment," Michelle said. "I'm not, like, a mean person, you know? We could have an actual conversation. Doesn't have to be super long or anything…"

"Guess what? I'm ignoring you."

"No, you're not."

"Yes, I am."

Michelle heaved a long sigh. "What sucks is that you used to be cool, right? And then you go acting all weird and stuff."

"Just leave me alone, okay?" I started fast-walking toward the entrance. Michelle lurched in front of me. Her friends hooted as we shuffled around, left, right. Left.

"There's this vegan place," she said. "It's literally next door. They've got empanadas."

"Vegan empanadas?"

Michelle pinned me against the wall, so close I smelled the "premium malt beverage" leaking out of her pores. "Man, you're so judgmental," she said.

She's the one who was judging.

"So, we're doing this or what?" Michelle clapped three times, like it was a magic trick.

If only she would disappear.

Okay. Confession time. I was this close to saying yes, I'll go with you to this empanada place, follow you just like your brainless dog.

I didn't want to be her dog anymore.

Michelle stood there, waiting for me to humiliate myself. The first band was warming up. I could feel the bass rumble all the way from the parking lot—a stuttery solo. It sounded like a conversation that couldn't get started.

"I'm kind of seeing someone," I lied.

Michelle's face crumpled. "God, Trenton. How long has this been going on?"

"Long enough."

"So basically you cheated on me." She was shouting now. A guy with a cast on his arm waddled past and stared at us.

"How is it 'cheating' if we're not together anymore?"

"Did we ever really break up?" she asked. "Like, officially?"

"I'm making it official now."

"You sure about that?"

"We're done."

She actually looked hurt. "I can take a hint."

"I'm not hinting. I'm telling you. Let's just be friends, okay? We never should've crossed that line. It was a total mistake."

"Was it?"

Now I felt guilty all over again.

Why couldn't I just make up my mind? I kept jumping back and forth, trying to decide. Was it really over? And to be totally honest, is that what I wanted?

"Unbelievable," I said. "Look at you, acting all innocent."

"What's her name? Do I know this girl?" Michelle sounded desperate now. I almost felt sorry for her. The key word is "almost."

"Her name's Pippa."

Oh shit. Where did that come from?

"So, if this is your girlfriend or whatever," she said, "why are you flying solo?"

I snatched what was left of the blunt and flicked it away. "Actually, I should call her."

"Yeah." Michelle nodded. "You should."

My hands trembled as I reached for the cell in my back pocket. Punched in the numbers. Held my breath.

"Nobody home?" Michelle was laughing at me, like always. Giving me that look. Waiting for me to fail.

The phone rang and rang. Finally, it clicked to voice-mail. Pippa's voice floated into my ear:

Leave your message at the beep.

My message.

"Um…" I tried to think of something. "I'm at Churchill's."

Michelle was giggling like crazy. I'm sure she hoped Pippa would hear it, too. Everybody in whole damn parking lot could hear it, judging by their stares. My brilliant solution? Keep talking.

"Hey. What's up, girl?" I mumbled into the phone, making sure to emphasize the final syllable, *girl*. "I'm about to dip. You still going out tonight?"

"That's called stalking." Michelle smirked.

"I'll be in the back. You know. Near the patio area where they play old movies and stuff. Call me when you get here." I shoved the phone in my pocket.

Michelle finally stopped giggling. "Do you really know this person? Sounded pretty casual. Not girl-friendy at all. More like a friend."

"Can't you be friends with your girlfriend?" That's what I wanted to find out.

"You didn't even say goodbye," she added.

"I'm saying it now."

"You're what?"

"Goodbye, Michelle." I couldn't look at her. This was so much harder than I'd thought. My throat was stinging. I kept my gaze locked on Second Avenue, where a cop car had rolled up. Great. Just what I needed, a visit from the fake I.D. squad. I wasn't going inside now.

As I walked away from the spinning lights, I felt a breeze of movement. Michelle lunged for my hat. She yanked it off my head and tossed it into the street, where it flopped like roadkill. I scooped it up and combed the ratty fur with my fingers, scraping off the dirt. Then I tugged it over my eyes.

five

Monday morning, I skipped class to hang out in the Hole—this empty lot next to campus. It wasn't much of a hole. More like a slope where everybody spread out beach towels and pretended to study. It was a prime spot for other activities, too, judging by the Philly Blunt papers smashed in the dirt.

I really messed up last night. Big time. What the hell was I thinking? I kept flashing back to the crazy message I'd left on Pippa's cell. I was so freaked out, I didn't have the balls to show up for film class. Not the smartest move, because I was already falling behind.

School was background noise. I'd do anything to escape it. But whenever I was stuck at home with Dad, there was no escape. You could never tell what kind of mood he'd be in. And if he was drinking, like usual, I stayed away. Otherwise I'd get blasted with his dark energy.

God knows I had enough of my own.

Dark energy is this secret force in the universe. Basically, it's everywhere, pushing stuff deeper into space. Sometimes when Dad was going off and I couldn't sleep at night, I'd take a walk around the backyard and look up at the sky. I tried to imagine all those galaxies spinning farther away. The Everglades is so thick with stars, it feels like it couldn't ever run out of light.

I decided that maybe I should try harder. At least, I owed it to Pippa. She didn't deserve to fail this stupid class because of me.

When lunchtime finally rolled around, half the school was in line for the vending machines. Everybody took a long time, trying to decide which artificially flavored soda to waste money on. I couldn't think about food. I had to talk to Pippa. That's all I needed.

A couple minutes later, I spotted her leaving the auditorium. She was trying to balance her camera bag, along with that doodle-crusted notebook she carried like it was part of her and she couldn't let it go.

I found a seed pod in the grass and tossed it in her direction. We used to throw them at each other on the playground. The hard, grenade-like shells made good ammunition.

"What's up, homeslice?" I said, adjusting the flaps on my trapper hat.

Pippa flopped next to me on the lawn. "Haven't seen you all day," she said. "That's crazy. I mean, the office is probably freaking out, right? You missed a lot of stuff in class. We learned how to take light readings."

"There's more light out here."

She laughed. "Well, I guess we can call off the search party."

"Hey, I'm always down for a party."

I didn't say anything about Churchill's or the fact that she never called back. No use talking about it. We sat in the Hole, listening to the lawn mower rumble past the auditorium. My eyes were burning. I leaned back, like I was going to take a nap.

"This is so random," Pippa said. "Last night I was watching a YouTube documentary about vampire bats. They don't suck blood, by the way. They lick it."

"That's good to know," I said.

"I got really into it. Then I couldn't fall asleep because I was so freaked out. I didn't notice that somebody had left a message on my cell."

Pippa held up her phone. The caller on the screen was listed as *TRENTOSCEO*. Guess the last few letters got cut off. It reminded me of Mom's anti-anxiety meds, those bottles with the really long names you can't pronounce.

Here's the saddest part.

I couldn't remember what I'd said.

What if it was really bad? After knocking back a couple beers, there's no telling what could come out of my mouth.

"At first, I thought it was people from school. You know. Crank calling me or whatever." Pippa lowered her head.

"Does that ever happen?" Sure, I'd made a few crank calls back in junior high. Usually I dialed up this Mexican place and asked for pizza. Yeah, that was totally original.

"I get crank calls sometimes," Pippa said.

"For real? Why would anybody do that to you?"

She kept scraping the polish on her thumb, chipping away the sparkly black paint. "I don't know."

"Well, I wasn't crank calling your house. I swear."

"It's no big deal. I really don't feel like talking about it. To be honest, it hasn't happened in a while."

I knew this meant one thing: It *was* happening. Why would anybody target Pippa? She didn't go around creating drama (unlike half the girls in this school). She belonged in her own universe, far from their dark energy.

"Last night I was at Churchill's," I told her. "Actually, the parking lot at Churchills. The cops shut it down and I had to leave. Sorry I didn't call you again later. By the time I got back to the Rez, it was super late."

"What's it like on the reservation?" she asked.

"It's not that different from anywhere else. My uncle's been teaching me about Miccosukee stuff," I said. "We're supposed to go camping in the Everglades. No tents. Just a hammock and a chickee hut. You have to sleep high, in case the gators sneak up on you."

"Your family sounds amazing," she said. "How come you never talked about them before?"

"Do you actually care?" I yanked another handful of grass.

"Sorry for asking," she said.

It felt like everything I said was wrong. I took a deep breath. "Okay. Let's rewind this conversation and start over."

"So you're living with your dad now?" she asked.

I nodded. "My mom basically dumped me."

"Sounds awkward."

"You have no idea." I rubbed my forehead, as if scrolling through the pages in my mind.

"What about your dad?"

"My dad? He's got issues. No joke. My mom was dumb enough to put up with it for years."

"You never told me."

"That's because I hadn't met you yet. One day, Mom told me to grab my shit, whatever I could throw in a duffel bag. All my Legos, my Gundam action figures. God, I even tried to shove the PlayStation in there. Then she's like, 'You can't bring that goddamn thing with you.' And I started crying and freaking out. Pretty embarrassing, I guess."

"That's the last time you saw him?"

"Yeah, we stayed with my grandma in Fort Myers for a couple months, but she and Mom kept fighting about stupid stuff. Then my dad got his ass thrown in jail. Mom finally woke up. I was still too little to understand what was really going on. All I knew was, that's when we got our first real house … the one on our block."

Our block.

"How come you never talked about this?" she asked.

"Because it's nobody's business."

"Not even your best friend's?"

I winced. "Except you, homeslice. I know you won't go around spreading my business, right?"

"Right," she said softly. And I felt like she meant it. For real.

"So, I moved in with my dad on the Rez."

I was on a roll, venting with the speed of a machine gun. Guess it all came spilling out.

"You know how people always say, 'I wish I could go back in time'? Well, I want the opposite. I want a fast-forward button to the future."

When I finally stopped talking, the silence hovered around us, louder than anything I'd heard in a while.

"Do you think that's scientifically possible?" she asked.

"Of course. You just get in a spaceship and fly around a black hole for twenty years. When you get back, everybody you knew on planet Earth is old and you're basically still young."

"Sounds kind of lonely," she said.

"What if I go with you?"

Pippa smiled. "You sure? I mean, that's a major sacrifice. You'd be giving up a lot."

If I stayed forever young with Pippa, I didn't need anything in this world. Or any others.

We could make our own.

———

For the rest of the week, I skipped a lot of my classes but kept going to Filmmaking. Mr. Bones showed us a bunch of scenes from old movies. It would've been cool if he let us keep watching, but he turned off the DVD player and talked the whole time.

The last movie wasn't even in English, but it was my favorite. I'd never watched a film in another language. At first, it was kind of weird, trying to read the subtitles. Then I didn't think about it anymore. It was better than 3-D. No magic glasses required.

The movie had an emo title, *Loves of a Blonde.* There's this girl who's following a guy around. When she shows up at his house, he acts like she's not even there. She was invisible, which was something I understood.

I wanted to make a movie like that. I just didn't know how.

After the screening, Mr. Bones snapped on the lights and told us to write a "response." I scribbled out some existential B.S. about how the main character's tool of a boyfriend was cooler in her imagination. It's real life that lets us down.

Mr. Bones collected our papers. "Okay, ladies and germs. I want to take a look at your dailies."

"Dailies" was film-speak for "raw, unedited footage."

I reached inside my bag and found my flash drive. There it was. My raw footage.

Mr. Bones fired up the computer and cut the lights. "Who wants to go first?"

Of course, Pippa raised her hand. She was either really brave or really insane. Nobody could've thought of all the crazy angles she'd filmed, like a wide shot of the school auditorium bathed in fluorescent light. Then a face popped into the frame. He was looking straight into the camera (a major no-no).

It was me.

"The framing is good," Mr. Bones said. "But it looks stretched out." He tried to adjust the computer screen, but it froze and we had to wait for him to restart it. "I'm completely failing here with this thing," he said. "Okay. What's with all those scratches? Is that dirt on the lens?"

"I was filming him in the dark," Pippa said.

A few people giggled, as if she'd said something X-rated.

"It's not just about cutting his head off, okay?" Mr. Bones said, launching another round of giggles. "Feels crooked to me. Next time, level the tripod with a bubble, but also use your eyes."

"I always use my eyes," Pippa said.

"For a shot like this, you should lock the tripod," Mr. Bones said. "Now who's next?"

I raised my hand.

The computer whirred to life. Everyone shut up and turned around in their seats.

At first, it looked like I had shot nothing.

"Did you forget to take off the lens cap?" Mr. Bones asked.

God, I hope not.

After a few seconds of blackness, there was a burst of light. On the screen, a pair of blurry legs marched in extreme close-up.

Dad.

I could see him now, walking away from me. For some reason, the farther he moved, the clearer he became. I'd shot the footage the week before, just goofing off with the video camera while Dad posed like the Hulk in the kitchen. On the table behind him, a Miller bottle glinted in the setting sun.

"Nice beer," somebody whispered.

Just kill me now. Please. I'd gladly accept a heart attack, blood clot, snake bite, appendicitis.

All at the same time.

————————

After class, Pippa waited in the auditorium. When she spotted me, she bowed like a Harajuku schoolgirl.

"Greetings, oh master of the cinematic tracking shot." She smoothed her skirt. Underneath it were her legs, balanced on clunky heels. Or "wedges." Whatever they're called. Who cares? I'm into them.

Girls should wear skirts more often.

Pippa fiddled with a loose staple on her sleeve. "I really liked your dailies."

My face burned. "Yeah? Well, the guy in your footage deserves an Academy Award."

"Maybe I should've paid him." She smiled so wide, I couldn't help smiling too.

"That's illegal, you know," I said. "Filming someone without their permission."

We reached the lockers. Pippa's was on the bottom, almost level with the concrete floor. She spun the lock until it popped open. The door was plastered with stickers so faded they curled at the edges, along with doodles of Jack Skellington, his hollow eyes and zipper grin.

"So I'm going to jail now?" She dug around in the avalanche of wadded-up papers.

I busted out a laugh. Where did she come up with this stuff? This girl was so smart. And just a little off. In other words, exactly my style.

"Don't worry. I won't blow your cover," I told her.

"Pinkie swear?"

We linked digits, just like the old days.

"Good." She unfolded a crinkled doodle, then rescrunched it. "Because I'm broke and I can't bail myself out."

"Me neither. I've been working for my fam on the Rez, but I keep blowing all my tips on Meat Lover's pizza. If I don't feed myself, it won't happen."

She punched the locker shut. Behind us, a bunch of sophomore chicks were talking in Spanish. The only word I understood was *loco*.

"Was that your dad?" Pippa asked. "I mean, the footage we saw in class."

I winced. "He's kind of unavoidable."

"I'd like to meet him."

"That's what you think." All I needed was for Pippa to swing by the house. Dad would probably talk smack about me. Or worse: creep her out with his amazing mack daddy skills.

"Actually, we have no choice. You're my partner. We're

supposed to be filming each other's 'family life,' remember? Unless you want to fail this class."

"I can't afford to fail. Thanks for reminding me."

"I should interview your dad," Pippa said. "Wouldn't that be amazing?"

No, actually it wouldn't. "Aren't we supposed to avoid 'talking head' interviews?" I asked.

"This could be a voiceover. Bet he's got a lot of stories."

"True," I said. "But here's the deal. Nobody wants to hear it."

"What makes you say that?"

"Because we live on a reservation in the middle of the Everglades. On weekends, my dad plays Early Bird bingo in the Game Lodge. How's that for your documentary? A real life Miccosukee tribesman. Or maybe you prefer something more exciting, like alligator wrestling?"

"Sounds good," she said. "But I might need to borrow a zoom lens."

The bell clanged and everybody bolted for the stairs. I stood back and watched them stumble over each other. What had I gotten myself into? I couldn't let Pippa see how pathetic my life had become. It was just too humiliating.

"Where are you headed now?" God, I sounded like a stalker.

"Computer Basics," she said. "Actually, it's not too basic. This kid, Sean, was supposed to teach me the magic of 'cascading style sheets' so I don't screw up this quiz. I emailed him a million times but he never wrote back."

The computer lab was on the other side of auditorium: a long, concrete slab facing the football field. We walked across the grass together. It was nice to get away from the endless rows of doors, all those numbers making you feel small.

We turned a corner and there was the building, rising up against the scalped-looking bushes. I had to do something. Fast.

"Let's just stay here," I said.

The Hole was looking worse than usual. I scooted around a shopping cart tipped upside down in the grass. Studied the plastic seat, with its X'd out pictures of smiling stick people: *HAZARDS CAN RESULT FROM IMPROPER BEHAVIOR.*

I tugged Pippa behind the cart. "Now we're invisible." *Playing pirates.*

The classrooms went blurry. I rubbed my face on my sleeve and peered through the cart's metal slats, trying to get a good look at who-knows-what.

We crouched there, not moving.

I bent a little closer, as if by gravitational pull, and kissed her, gently, on the lips.

Then something even more amazing happened.

Pippa kissed me back.

It happened so fast, I might've hallucinated the whole thing.

"Wait," I said as she scrambled away from me. Away from everything. I called her name, but she was already headed to class, her hands stuffed deep in her pockets.

six

When I got home from school, I couldn't stop thinking about Pippa's kiss. At first, I thought she was into it. Now I wasn't so sure. And if she really did feel that way, could it destroy the thing we'd found again?

Here's a bigger question:

Could we take that chance?

My ex was the second girl I'd ever kissed.

Pippa was the first.

Afterwards, we never talked about it. We were in fifth grade. It didn't mean anything. That's what I kept telling myself.

The kiss today replayed in my mind. Why did she pull away? We were at school, which made it kind of awkward. But nobody was around. No kissing police or pervy teachers with nothing better to do than hand out detentions. Guess she just wasn't prepared for it. Or maybe that was a lie I wanted to believe in. As long as I didn't think too hard, I could almost forget it.

On Saturday morning, I padded barefoot into the kitchen. When I squinted through the window, Uncle Seth was in the backyard, talking to a Miccosukee woman in a straw hat. He used to be married, but his wife died in a car accident a long time ago. Sometimes I wondered if he had a girlfriend. Not that I was the world's expert on that subject.

"You're up early," Dad said, drifting behind me.

"I'm working on a project," I told him. Code-speak for *none of your business.*

"What sort of project?"

"A film thing."

Dad nodded. "Another one of your Hollywood productions?"

"It's for school. Remember, they let me borrow that camera?"

"When is this 'film thing' due?" He filled the blender with a scoop of his weight-lifting mix—gritty packets of Muscle Juice that probably caused cancer in lab rats.

"Soon."

That's all he needed to know.

When I looked through the window again, Uncle Seth was gone. He'd probably snuck off with his boys to shoot hoops in the gym. Around here, basketball was kind of an obsession. I'd never seen anybody get so worked up over that game as the Rezzy kids. I swear, even the little babies were swagged out in Miami Heat gear before they could walk.

"Did Uncle Seth take the Ninja?" I asked.

The Ninja was my dad's bike—a sweet Kawasaki. He was on it every chance he got. I couldn't really blame the man.

Dad fired up the blender. "Don't think so."

"Can I borrow it? I'll bring it right back. Promise. I'll even put gas in the tank. It's running on fumes."

"Is it?" Dad shouted, punching a button, then another. The blender's noise got higher-pitched. It sounded like an airboat taking off. "Aren't you supposed to be working today?"

"Yeah," I yelled, like a nanosecond after Dad unplugged the stupid blender. I felt like an idiot for shouting. And I'd totally forgotten about my job at the gator show. Uncle Seth kept promising to teach me how to wrestle the gator, but so far, it wasn't happening.

Dad reached into a drawer and tossed me the car keys. "You can drive your own car. Forget about that bike. And by the way, I heard you missed work last time."

"Not even." I'd been a half hour late. That's not the same as missing work. I grabbed my jacket off the couch and headed for the door.

"What about breakfast?" He lifted his glass of Muscle Juice.

"That stuff will kill you, Dad. It's too healthy," I said, yanking open the fridge.

My dad never tossed stuff out, no matter how rotten it got. I'd learned to sniff the milk before splashing it on my Cheerios. The fridge was crammed with take-out boxes—so many there was no room left for real food. He even saved the chopsticks and soy sauce from the Chinese place, electric-colored packets decorated with pandas.

I found one of his Power Bars in the "crisper" drawer. "Candy, yes," I said, tearing off the wrapper.

"Trent."

I turned around to face him.

"Found some stuff in your room."

Stuff?

"Don't bring girls over to the house," Dad said.

I figured he was talking about Michelle. He made it sound like I was getting nonstop action (not even close). It was totally unfair, the way he was judging me. Did he go in my room and search for evidence? As I turned away, he grabbed my shoulder. I fell backward against the wall and the granola bar shot across the floor.

"You hear what I said?"

He was starting to freak me out. "Yeah," I muttered. "No girls. I heard you."

I jerked free of Dad's grip. Then I picked up the stupid granola bar. *Supports muscle strength*, the label said.

It took, like, five seconds to run outside and unlock the car. My hands shook as I cranked the ignition. I sped past a row of concrete houses and turned in front of the Welcome Center. In the middle of the parking lot was a giant statue of a Miccosukee guy tickling an alligator's chin. I wanted to push it into the canal.

My dad talked about being "Indian," but if he ever knew anything about "the old ways," he forgot a long time ago. I got dumped here because my mom didn't want me around. And she didn't want Dad around, either.

Not that I blamed her.

———

Driving to Miami, I sat behind the wheel and punched buttons on the radio. Broken lyrics floated out, telling me things I didn't believe. I left it on a Spanish station. All those lies sounded a lot better when I couldn't understand the words.

My old neighborhood was kind of boring compared to the Rez. All the houses looked the same in the morning light. No crazy paint colors. And it was mad quiet. Everybody stayed locked indoors all day, glued to the TV, watching shows about so-called reality.

I kept going past the gated houses and spiked metal fences—whether keeping people out or in, it was hard to tell. As I pulled onto my block, I thought about rolling up to Mom's house. Then I saw a car I recognized in the driveway.

What the hell was I thinking? I shoved another chunk of granola in my mouth. If I was going to survive this weekend, I needed all the muscle strength I could get.

I parked next to the rusty swingset at Pippa's, got out, and walked to the porch. On the steps were a bunch of plastic lids filled with cat food and ants. All the flowers were in various stages of death. There was even a pile of faded paperbacks spilling out of a Hefty bag. My mom would've killed me if I left a book outside.

Maybe Pippa didn't live here anymore?

It seemed totally possible. Her mom got divorced back when I was in middle school. I glanced at the window by the front door. There was so much junk piled against the glass, I couldn't get a decent look. Only one thing left to do.

I knocked on the door. Waited. Knocked again.

Yeah, maybe I should've called first.

The door swung open. Pippa's mom stood there, wearing a T-shirt that said *Boss of Floss*.

"Is Pippa around?" I asked.

"Wow, kiddo. What a surprise. I saw your mother at Costco. When was it? Let's say, last week. Looked like she'd frosted her hair. How's she doing?"

"Um. I have no idea," I mumbled.

"And why is that?"

"Because I'm staying at my dad's place now."

"Where?"

"Highway forty-one. Just off the turnpike."

"Near the Everglades, you mean?" Pippa's mom was still clueless.

"In it, actually," I said.

She stepped out onto the porch and pushed something across the boards with her toes. "I'm sweating bullets. Let's move away from the sun. Want anything, sweetie? I could nuke some coffee. You take unleaded?" Her word for decaf.

"Sounds good. All I had for breakfast was a Power Bar. It wasn't very powerful."

I followed her inside. The kitchen was crammed with

water bottles and empty cat food bags, folded neatly and tucked near the stove. Don't get me wrong. The place was clean. It was just ... cluttered.

When Pippa came into the kitchen, I figured she'd be surprised.

She blinked at me. "Trent? Why are you here?"

Not exactly the reaction I wanted.

"I thought we were ... you know. Working on that film thing," I said.

Pippa didn't say anything. It was hard to see her face because the house was really dark. And there was so much crap everywhere, it looked like a yard sale in the living room.

"So you're helping Pippa with a film project?" her mom wanted to know.

"Our project," I said. "We're making documentaries."

"What are you documenting, exactly?"

I thought for a second. "Life."

The microwave beeped and I almost jumped out of my skin. Let's just say the whole situation was kind of awkward. Pippa still wasn't talking. Her mom kept rattling stuff in the cabinets, trying to find a coffee mug.

"That's okay, Mom," Pippa finally said, grabbing her camera bag. "We should get going."

"Pippa drinks way too much caffeine anyway," her mom said, like she wasn't even there. "Coffee leeches the calcium in your teeth. Good thing you eat a lot of cheese."

"We're leaving. Now." Pippa laced up her combat boots.

As we headed outside, I couldn't keep up with her. She was fast-walking to the car, not even looking at me.

"Well, I guess we're filming my life, then," I said. "You sure I can't shoot some footage here? Since we're already at your place and everything?"

Pippa shook her head. "Not unless you're making an episode of *Hoarders*."

She was embarrassed. God, why didn't I see it before?

"Your house isn't on that level yet," I said. "We don't need to call an intervention."

I thought this would make her laugh. Of course, I was wrong.

"It's been like this since Dad left," Pippa told me. "Sometimes I'm scared that my mom has mental problems. She thinks we're all going to die in a hurricane. You saw the water bottles, right? And I'm sure you noticed the boards on our windows."

Actually, I didn't notice the boards. I did notice that it was dark as hell.

"That's a good thing," I said, unlocking the passenger door. "Why?"

"Now you're ready for the zombie apocalypse."

She smiled. "What if I'm the only survivor?"

"You mean I really can't come over?" I asked. "That's so not fair, homeslice."

"I'll have to think about it," she said.

"So it's like that, huh?"

Pippa dumped her camera bag in the backseat. "Oh my god, you still have that tape?" She pointed at *The Magic of Muscle Singing*.

"It's my mom's tape, actually. It's probably older than this car."

"Classic," Pippa said. "I'm totally stealing it."

We both made a grab for it at the same time. My hand fumbled down near her legs.

"Sorry about the groping," I said, sitting up straight.

"I'll survive." She pushed the tape into the deck and hit play. A vocal coach started chanting, "My mother made me mash my M&Ms." Then he clicked his tongue like he was part dolphin.

"I like tapes and records more than CDs anyway," Pippa said. "Why do they sound so much better?"

"Because CDs are too perfect. You don't hear any scratches or pops between songs."

"The scratches definitely make it interesting," she said. "More like real life."

I laughed. "Real life has scratches?"

She cranked the volume. "You know what I mean."

Me and Pippa used to sing along in the car. Nothing could make me laugh like that—laugh until I actually peed my pants (embarrassing but true).

A couple minutes later, the tape clicked to the other side. Bass guitar notes dribbled out of the speakers.

"What is this music?" Pippa asked, closing her eyes. "It's actually kind of good."

"It's nothing." I hit the eject button.

"Wait. That's you playing bass?"

"I wanted it to sound 'vintage' so I recorded over a tape."

"Can I have a copy of that song?"

"It's not a song yet. But I could make it happen."

"Yeah?" she said. "I think you should."

She rewound the tape back to the beginning. For the rest of the drive, we listened in silence, and that was cool with me.

———————

When we got to the Welcome Center, Pippa headed straight for the gift shop. *HALF OFF TODAY ONLY*, a sign said, as if the day itself were on sale. I couldn't understand why she wanted to film a pile of back-scratchers made of dried-up gator claws.

"So, when are we interviewing your dad?" Pippa asked.

That was the last thing I wanted to do. "You should film the gator show," I said. "It's starting soon."

I glanced down the aisles. A little girl bolted past me, screaming words I didn't understand. She carried a snow globe in both hands. Inside it, Santa's sleigh floated above a beach, pulled by a team of flamingoes.

"You guys want to see some alligator wrestling?" somebody asked.

Uncle Seth.

I recognized his laugh, the way he poured his whole body into it.

Pippa was so excited she did a little robot dance, right in the middle of the gift shop. It was kind of cute, actually. I was still trying to figure out how to keep her away from the drama that had become my life.

Uncle Seth was in his wrestling gear. He wore a patchwork vest and his bare feet were dusted with sand. A necklace of snaggly teeth bounced against his chest as he loped toward me.

"And I believe you're supposed to be helping out today?" He steered me outside.

We walked toward a clump of chickee huts facing a sandy pit. I was thankful for the shade. Already, my T-shirt had begun to stick to my shoulder blades. On the other side of a chain-link fence, an alligator sprawled in a concrete pool. He looked like a deflated truck tire. At least until he cracked his mouth wide open.

"Why is he yawning?" Pippa asked.

"It's a she, actually," said Uncle Seth. "And she's just cooling off. That's how they regulate their body temperature."

I wiped my face on my sleeve. "Wish I could regulate mine."

Uncle Seth unlocked a gate and disappeared somewhere behind the sand pit. Then it was just me and Pippa and the gator. I was still waiting when a crowd started to press against the fence. A lady asked if I knew where to find the vending machines.

"Hot as balls out here," she said, lighting up a cigarette. "I could really use a Diet Coke."

I felt kind of stupid, just standing around with a bunch

of tourists. They pointed their cameras at the pool, but the gator didn't twitch. A pack of teenaged boys took turns rattling the fence.

"It's not even alive," one of them muttered. "What a rip-off."

If I pushed him over the fence, he would find out if the gator was alive.

A loudspeaker crackled and an announcement boomed like the voice of God: *The show will be starting soon. If you have small children, please make sure they are seated away from the fence.*

"Are you going in there?" Pippa asked.

"My uncle won't let me wrestle yet. I just collect the tips at the end."

She took the camera out of its case. "This is so amazing. I can't wait to film some action shots. It will so get me an A on this project."

Most of the girls in the audience were slumped in the back row, playing with their cell phones. Pippa moved right up front. She propped the camera real close to the fence. Then my uncle came out and everybody clapped, although nothing had happened yet.

He took hold of the gator's tail and dragged her into the middle of the sand pit. The gator was hissing like crazy. You could tell the audience was freaking out. Everybody shoved their cameras against the chain-link. Some girl behind me kept saying, "Oh my god," every five seconds.

Uncle Seth crouched down in the sand. He stroked and tapped the gator's nose until her mouth sprang open.

"This is how I keep my nails trim." Uncle Seth shoved his hand in the narrow space between the gator's jaws. He jumped back just before her teeth clamped shut, igniting a round of shrieks from the crowd.

His next trick was even more awesome. He snuck up behind the gator and crouched on her back. The gator didn't seem too happy. She thrashed her tail back and forth, making angel wings in the sand. Slowly, Uncle Seth tilted her massive head toward his throat, then tucked the tip of her snout under his chin. He stayed like that for a minute, lifting both hands as if saying, "I surrender."

I leaned against the chain-link fence. You could see the gator's rubbery lips, speckled with something like beard stubble. Uncle Seth brought his hands down and untucked his chin.

"I'll do it again," he said, "just in case you missed your photo opportunity."

This time, he squatted behind the gator's head. When she cracked her jaws apart, he slid his face in there. Everybody gasped like a fake TV sound effect. Except it wasn't fake. Neither was my uncle's stunt. I didn't even see him let go. He jumped backward, stumbling a little as his feet kicked arcs of sand.

The crowd oohed and ahhed, right on cue. Then Uncle Seth talked about the Miccosukee people, their hands-free style of wrestling, the skill it took to rope a gator and trade its skin for guns. Nobody listened. They were too busy gathering their purses and wheeling away strollers. A lady took out her cell and blabbed at ear-piercing decibels. "I can't hear you," she kept shouting. "Can you hear me? What do you mean, 'Not really'? How about now?"

I tuned the volume down inside my mind so I wouldn't have to listen. All I heard was my breath, like a hurricane's pulse, until the only thing left was silence.

seven

"So tell me the truth," Pippa said. "Your uncle wasn't faking it, right? I mean, putting his life in danger so a bunch of tourists could have a Kodak moment."

I'd collected the tips and we were back in the parking lot. The breeze had picked up, carrying a hint of smoke. I always liked that smell, especially when it floated from somewhere far away, the burn you couldn't see.

"This isn't a joke," I said.

The sun was in Pippa's eyes, making her squint like she was hatching evil plans. "I just meant—"

"It's part of my culture," I told her. "Didn't you hear what he said at the show?"

"For your information, I *was* listening. In fact, I was probably the only one listening."

"Oh, thanks. That makes me feel better."

"What the hell is wrong with you? I'm in the middle of freaking nowhere, just for this project."

"Is that the only reason you came?" I asked.

Pippa reached into her bag and pulled out her sunglasses. The plastic frames were sprinkled with pirate skulls. "Geez, Trent. What do you want me to say?"

"I wouldn't call this nowhere."

"Okay. Fine. I guess everywhere is somewhere."

I tried to laugh, but it came out high-pitched and jumpy. "You're wrong," I said, tapping my forehead. "It's all in the mind."

Pippa was definitely a weird girl. I wanted to get close to her again, but she kept blocking me out. In the distance, a car honked one long note that stretched and faded. There was nothing on the horizon, which circled us for miles. Just the chickee huts and a cloudless sky so bright it hurt to look at it.

"Where are you going?" Pippa asked.

I told her the truth. "Nowhere."

———

"Everybody lives close to their families," I said as we drove through the Rez. "It's all divided by clans."

We passed the burger shack right across from the Rez school, made a couple turns, and pulled up to the Little Blue House.

"So how come you didn't grow up around here?" Pippa asked.

"Because of my mom," I said. "She's not Indian, remember?"

Pippa was quiet for a moment. "Does that mean you're not part of the tribe?" she asked.

I turned off the radio. "Depends on who you ask."

Next door at Uncle Seth's, the elder ladies were having a yard sale. The aunts had set up tables on the grass, each loaded with beaded necklaces, miniature canoes, and paper plates stacked with fry bread. We parked and walked over.

Pippa grabbed the camera and started filming. She was really getting into it, practically kneeling down to get the best angle.

"What's this thing?" She held up a skinny wooden racket.

"That's for playing stickball," I explained. "It's super old-school. Nobody really does it anymore. It's kind of like lacrosse."

"Have you ever played it?"

I put the racket back on the table. "Nobody does. That's what I just said."

Maybe I was making her uncomfortable. Actually, I was the one getting weirded out. It wasn't because people stared (and, of course, they did). Everybody was really nice. The aunts nodded at me, but they didn't talk to Pippa. Maybe it was a mistake, bringing her here.

"They probably think I'm your girlfriend," she said.

My face heated up. I looked down and hoped she didn't notice.

"Are we going to your dad's house or what?" Pippa asked.

I didn't want to deal with him. Not after his little freakout this morning. At the same time, I was like, why can't I bring somebody over? I live here too.

"It's part of my uncle's place, actually. Or, my aunt's, but she passed on. See, this is how it goes. When a guy gets married, he moves into his wife's house. Basically, women run the show. They even get to pick your names."

"Names?"

"You get a 'baby name' when you're born. Only your mom knows the real name. When boys grow into men, they have a naming ceremony. It's supposed to mean you're an adult or whatever."

"Girls don't get a new name?"

I shrugged. "They don't need it."

"So when are you getting yours?"

I unlocked the door to the Little Blue House and kicked it open. All around the door frame were metal sculptures: a half-moon and a smiling sun, along with a polka-dotted lizard.

"My what?" I asked.

"Your grown-up name."

"Oh." I flicked on the lights. "Most guys my age have theirs already."

"This is a big deal, right? The ceremony, I mean."

"Yeah, but I'm not in the tribe, officially. So it won't be happening. Not for me, anyway."

"Maybe you can find a way in," Pippa said.

"Maybe." I didn't really feel like talking about it.

"Is there, like, a test? Do you have to study for this naming thing?" she wanted to know.

"You get to decide when you're ready."

"That's cool," she said.

"When you start asking questions, the elders say you're good to go. It's all about learning the songs. We've got a whole encyclopedia of them. Like, there's songs to find herbs. Songs for hiding and protection. Songs to make people happy. You just have to memorize them."

"That wouldn't be too hard. Music was always your special talent."

"Yeah, well, I'm not so special anymore. That's why I need to pass this class, right? For the win."

Pippa sank onto the couch and sort of collapsed into me. I'm sure she was just tired, but it felt weirdly familiar, leaning against her. Weird in a good way. I kept glancing at the door, thinking Dad would bust in here, but he was probably getting wasted. The usual Saturday routine.

"Let's get some B-roll footage." I took out the camera and aimed it at my open mouth. "I'm documenting my wisdom teeth before they get ripped out."

"You're not smart enough to have wisdom teeth."

"Don't say mean things to me. I might cry."

"Aren't we supposed to be making movies about real life?"

"This is real life." I lifted my Native Pride T-shirt and pointed the camera at my stomach. "Now I'm documenting my appendix scar."

"Gross. If I fail, it's all your fault."

I dumped the camera back in its case. "This thing is a piece of crap. It won't even turn on. And the batteries look dead."

"You can't tell by looking," Pippa said. "Did you charge the extra batteries?"

"Was I supposed to?"

Pippa sighed. "We can't film anything else until it charges."

Okay. Now we had to charge the stupid batteries. I needed to get Pippa out of the house before Dad got back.

"Come on," she said. "Pass me the worksheet. We have to make a shot list."

"A shit list?"

"Oh, you're so funny I forgot to laugh." She gave me a push and my skin heated up again. I looked down at my sneakers, the thumbtack wedged in my heel. Maybe if I pried it out, I would fly around the room like a balloon.

"Let's work in the kitchen," I told her. At least if Dad pulled up in the driveway, I would spot him through the window.

The kitchen looked like it had been attacked by velociraptors. PlayStation games were scattered all over the table, along with a flattened bag of chips. Neon orange crumbs were smashed deep into a place mat. I flipped it over, finding a half dozen pennies and a wrinkled magazine—*Winds of Change: Your Number One Source for Indigenous News.*

Pippa wanted something to eat, so I wasted fifteen minutes trying to microwave a Hot Pocket.

"I really can't afford to fail this class," she said.

"Yo. Chill," I said, licking the grease off my fingers. "Got it covered. Out of everything I'm taking this semester, it's like the only class I really care about."

"That's sad," Pippa said.

"Know what's even sadder? I'm probably going to drop out anyway."

"You mean, drop out of Filmmaking?"

"Out of everything."

"I won't let you," she said. "That's not going to happen. Swear?" She held up her fists. "Or I'll have to track you down and kill you."

"Okay. I'm freaking out now." I laughed.

"I didn't hear you swear."

"I swear all the time. It's a bad habit."

Pippa got all serious. "I mean it. For real. You can't drop out of school. You're too smart."

"Just a second ago, you were saying the opposite."

"Why are you giving up so easily?"

"I'm not."

"Well, that's what it looks like," she said, frowning. "You always had better grades than me. You didn't even study. That's what got me so mad."

"Yeah, well. Maybe I stopped caring."

"So what happened? Is there a reason you don't care anymore? Or is it just easier?"

"What's easier?" I asked.

"Not caring."

She didn't understand. It was a lot harder pretending *to* care.

"School feels like a big waste of time right now," I told her. "Even when I was trying to work on my music, it all seemed so fake. When you're a kid, everybody says, 'You can be anything you want.' But that's a total lie."

"I know what you mean," she said. "My mom is always going on about my GPA, like, if I just work hard enough, I'll be set for life. But there's so many amazing things I want to do. Like, I have this master plan. I'm going to direct music videos, right? And make horror movies and stuff. But let's be real. Most of that will probably never happen."

When I heard Pippa say that, I felt really bad. "Don't let that noise get into your head. You just have to go for it."

"Really?" she said.

"I believe in you," I said. And that was the truth.

Pippa covered her face with her hands. "Now you're making me feel all awkward," she said, peeking between her fingers.

Could this girl be any cuter?

"Okay, Mr. Rock Star," she said. "We need to get back to work."

"Didn't we shoot enough today?" I asked.

"We haven't interviewed your dad yet."

"Trust me. He's not worth interviewing." On the kitchen counter, Dad had left a boom box. I scanned past a bunch of Spanish stations and settled on Power 96. "'Big Pimpin'.' Yeah, that's how I roll. This song describes my life."

"Seriously. I don't think this is a difficult a concept to grasp."

"My pimp hand? I keep it strong, player."

"Let's wait until your dad gets back. You can hold the

camera while I ask questions. I'll edit it with the footage from the gator show. Like a montage or something."

"Mr. Bones said no 'talking head' stuff."

"It won't be talking head. I could do a voiceover."

"Methinks thou art cheating, fair maiden," I said in a fake British accent. I opened the fridge, took out a can of Reddi-wip, and sprayed it into my mouth. "Nice. This thing's down to fumes."

"Is it weird living with your dad?" Pippa asked. "I mean, does it feel weird because you didn't grow up on the reservation?"

"What is this? You're interviewing me now?"

"Off the record," she said.

"Yeah, it feels weird. I don't even know my dad really well. Mom always talked shit about him. I guess in my mind, I had this idea he'd be different. That living here would be different. Actually, the Rez is pretty chill. Nobody acts like I'm a freak because I'm not in the tribe."

"And you want to be in it?" she asked quietly.

"Let me check on those zombie batteries. See if they've risen from the dead," I muttered, ducking out of the kitchen. Why was it so hard to answer her questions? I didn't have answers. At least, none that Pippa needed to hear.

The tribe had its own rules. That's the way it had to be.

My mom told me that Dad couldn't wait to leave the Rez. As soon as he got out of school, he moved into his own place with some bandmates. He probably thought he was going to be famous. Guess he never planned on me showing up. He didn't plan on a lot of things.

The camera batteries were plugged into the wall behind the dining room table. I had to squeeze behind it to pull them out and that's when I saw the gun—smaller and more compact than my air rifle. I picked up the .357 Mag and felt its weight in my hands.

Dad liked to go to Trail Glades on the weekend and fire off rounds at paper targets. He was always telling me that we'd go shooting together. Of course, that never happened. Now the gun was sitting next to a stack of bills. The safety was locked. I found the carrying case—a soft, padded bag that looked like a fanny pack—unzipped on a chair.

I figured Dad had gone shooting earlier and left it on the table. Pretty typical. I fit the Mag back in its case. Now what? I felt kind of weird about it being out in the open. Meanwhile, Pippa was talking to me, but I couldn't hear her. Without thinking, I shoved the gun in my backpack and zipped it.

"What's going on with the batteries?" she asked.

"All charged up." I grabbed a set of keys off the table. Then I had a brilliant idea. "Ever been on a motorcycle?"

"Lots of times," she said. "Okay. I lied."

"My dad's got this Kawasaki. The engine runs kind of chunky. I think it needs the plugs changed, but he's too lazy to deal with it."

"Is that your half-assed version of an invite?"

"You might say that." I spun the keys. "Besides. You could shoot a ton of amazing road footage."

"Oh, I get it. You mean, like, those old movies where people are driving, right? And the road is, like, projected behind their heads?"

"Pretty much," I said, throwing on my jacket.

She jabbed her thumb at my Scout badge: *ON MY HONOR. TIMELESS VALUES.* "Is that supposed to be ironic?"

"There should be a zombie survival badge," I said.

"Oh my god. That would be awesome. 'Hey, I've been working on this zombie movie with my friend Trent. We do all our own stunts and everything—'"

"A zombie wouldn't have a chance around a crocodile," I cut in. "Crocs have a thing for dead meat, you know? Nice and soft. If it's too tough to eat now, they'll store it for later. See, they're different from gators. They're kind of like the vultures of the swamp."

"I guess that's one way of looking at it," Pippa said.

"Did you know that vultures defend themselves by projectile vomiting? Can you imagine sneaking up on one and he's all freaked out and just lets loose on you, like, take that!"

Pippa followed me into the garage. It was so packed with junk, you almost missed the lime-green motorcycle tipped against the wall.

"The kickstand's busted," I said. "It's a sweet bike, though. My dad treats it like garbage."

"And he doesn't care if you steal it?"

"Steal? It's called borrowing." I lifted the seat and took out a helmet, which was like something an astronaut would wear. "It's all good. Mucho good, in fact," I said, passing it to her. "This will keep your zombie brains from splattering all over the concrete."

"Thanks." Pippa slid the helmet on. It was way too big for her, but she looked totally badass. Not to mention, super cute.

I grinned. "You ready?"

eight

The pavement flew beneath us. We were going faster than the cars, zipping in and out of lanes. It was just me and Pippa and the bike. All the pines on the side of the road smushed together like backgrounds in cartoons.

As we picked up speed, my T-shirt flapped against my skin. I was freaking out. Not gonna lie. When I gunned the engine, my pulse jumped. No going back now. Pippa wrapped her arms around the space above my jeans and squeezed.

We were totally in the open. No protection if we wiped out. The bike rumbled under me like it might burst into flames. That would be cool, but not exactly convenient.

We rode to Everglades National Park and rolled straight through the entrance. Just waved as we passed the ranger station. The guy inside waved back. I kept cruising down this wide, curvy path. There was nobody around except for a lonely backpacker marching into the swamp.

"This is the perfect place for my zombie movie," Pippa screamed into the wind.

"The army used to hide missiles out here," I told her.

She wasn't really listening. That's when I pulled off the road.

Pippa squeezed tighter. "We're stopping?"

I glanced at the sky. Vultures circled like punctuation marks. I remembered what I'd told Pippa. They defended themselves by vomiting. Nature was so weird.

"Don't you want to check it out?" I asked.

"Check what out?"

"The abandoned missile base."

"Okay." I could tell she was trying to hold it together. "Are there any snakes around?"

"Burmese pythons, mostly."

She shuddered. "Lots of them?"

"Trust me. You don't want to know. Even the park rangers lost count. That's because stupid people buy them as pets. When the python grows to be, like, twelve feet long, they throw them away. Kind of messed up. I mean, it's not the snake's fault…"

I swung my leg over the bike. Pippa almost fell, but I helped her down like a true gentleman.

"Watch out for the tailpipe," I said, grabbing a backpack from under the seat. "The metal gets so hot, you could torch the skin off your leg. That's what happened to my dad. Third-degree burns. He's got a scar and everything."

The stripes in the pavement were so faded, I wondered

how long ago anybody had driven over them. We walked to a fence snarled with barbed wire. Behind it, a sign said: *U.S. ARMY RESTRICTED AREA. USE OF DEADLY FORCE IS AUTHORIZED.*

"This is crazy." Pippa was talking so fast, it sounded like she was on crack. "Oh my god. I can't believe we're doing this. Are you sure we won't get caught?"

I was already climbing the fence. I tossed my jacket over the barbed wire so Pippa wouldn't get cut. She hauled herself over like it was nothing. It took me a couple tries just to dig my sneakers into the links without slipping.

Once I reached the top, I was super proud of myself. No joke.

Getting down was another thing.

"Now what?" I shouted.

"Just move fast and don't think."

"I'm not very good at that."

"Which one? Moving fast? Or thinking?"

"Both. There's a certain part of my anatomy that … um … I don't want to mess up." Did I just say that out loud?

I managed to scramble over the barbed wire. Once I was halfway down the other side, I jumped and hit the ground so hard a jolt of pain blasted through my knees.

"Nice," Pippa said. "Are you just going to leave the bike there?"

"Oh, right. The swamp apes might steal it. Quit your bitching. Nobody's gonna find it."

The road curved toward a building in the distance. The

missile base was just a row of cement blocks, like the ones we used to stack in the backyard, pretending we were Storm Troopers defending the Death Star. This thing was for real, though it was all boarded up with plywood and the bolts in the *DANGER* sign had rusted.

A burnt-looking tree was the only semi-living thing in sight. Pippa took a composition book out of her bag. She sat down, right there on the grass, and started writing. It was kind of geeky and adorable at the same time.

"Taking notes?" I asked.

"For my zombie screenplay. I want to remember what this place looks like. It's kind of epic."

"I used to write stuff down," I told her. "Song lyrics, mostly. But my mom tossed all my old notebooks."

"That's so evil."

I shrugged. "Evil is too kind a word."

"You should keep writing."

"True. I've been working on new lyrics. Nothing major. Just getting some random ideas. Music is my ultimate release. It's like a VIP screening in my brain."

"A song is like a movie, too."

"How so?"

"It's there. You're in the moment. Then it's gone."

Nobody had ever talked about stuff like that with me. I wanted to keep talking to Pippa...tell her about the music and the words that kept me awake at night.

"Sometimes I think I've found the perfect melody," I explained, "and after playing it for a while, it doesn't feel right anymore. Or it maybe sounded better in my head. Or I'm just not good enough to play it."

"I know what you mean," Pippa said. "When I listen to an awesome song on the radio, it feels like the band is singing with me."

"My ex-girlfriend, Michelle, always made fun of my songs. Actually, she thought they were all about her."

What the hell was I saying? This was the perfect time to shut up. Any rational person would've stopped talking. Did I?

Of course not.

"Can I tell you something personal?" I asked.

"Sure," Pippa said, staring up at the trees.

"Michelle was my first. I mean, you'll always remember your first, right?"

"Yeah. I guess." She shoved the notebook in her bag. "Unless you were unconscious or something."

I stared.

"Sorry. I was trying to be funny," she said.

"Thanks. That really helps."

"I mean, I know what you're going through."

"You do?"

She hugged me. When she started to pull away, I didn't let go. Pippa was looking at me so intensely I forgot to breathe. We kissed right there on the abandoned road, a place where men had built missiles and planned wars, and now, hardly anybody remembered. She was breathing into me, daring me to feel something.

Still, I held back.

She must've noticed. Yeah, I'm sure she did. God. Why couldn't I be normal for once? I was overanalyzing the situation as usual, thinking about something my crazy cousin, Marco, had told me in back sixth grade: kissing seals the deal. Of course, I hadn't made out with anybody then. Not unless you count Pippa, who'd tried to "practice" on me during a marathon of Ninja Turtles.

Now we were kissing for real.

Shit.

I had officially lost it. Why was I thinking about anything at a time like this? I needed to focus. Here I was, alone with this girl who had somehow changed into this mega hottie, and I couldn't even kiss it away.

Pippa tilted her chin down, closing me off. She must've sensed that I was someplace else.

"What's wrong?" I whispered.

"Sorry. I'm a little nervous."

I stroked the small of her back, tracing circles there. "Do I make you nervous?"

"Only when you do that."

"I'll stop, if you want."

"Don't. I mean ... I don't want you to stop."

My hands slid inside her shirt. I kept mumbling stuff like, "You're so damn pretty." She told me to keep going. It seemed like the right thing to say. I wanted to feel good, too; but all I felt was confused. And to make things more confusing, I didn't know why.

On the side of the building, somebody had painted a rocket with the words *U.S. ARMY* printed in capital letters. Under it floated some modern day graffiti. *YUCK*, it said, beside a frowny face with a mouthful of fangs.

Pippa pushed my hands off her. Shoved me, actually. "Do you always kiss with your eyes open?"

"Huh?" I was still looking at the rocket.

"Just be real. Seriously. I can take a hint. If this is too weird—"

"It's not like that. I mean, shit. I'm sorry."

What was I sorry for? It seemed like I was always apologizing.

Pippa smoothed her hair into place, tucking a few strands behind her ears. "Let's just go, okay?"

"Wait. I want to show you something."

She was halfway to the fence. In other words, back to where we started. "I've seen enough."

"God, you're so judgmental. It's like you're trying to make yourself mysterious."

"That makes no sense, Trent. How can I 'make myself mysterious'? It's not like I'm pretending to be somebody different. Unlike other people I know."

"What's that supposed to mean?" Now I was getting pissed.

"This is so wrong." She grabbed a tissue from her bag and mashed it against her face.

"Talk to me for one second. Please."

"You're just using me to get over your ex," Pippa said.

"That's totally not true. Don't even play that." I reached

out for her, but she jerked away as if I were Kryptonite. "You're being really dramatic over nothing."

Great. Now she was full-on crying and, of course, it was my fault. I stood there thinking how cute she looked. I wanted to kiss her spiky eyelashes. Hold her until she stopped shaking.

"Can we go back now?" Pippa sniffed.

"Not until you see the best part," I said, stomping off toward a garage-type building just a few yards ahead. On the ground, you could see wing-shaped dents, as if something heavy had dragged across it a long time ago. So this was the abandoned missile base.

"There's a door," I said.

"Yeah, I can see that."

I jammed my pocketknife into the lock, gave the knob a few twists. Just like magic, it swung open.

"If you think I'm going in there, you're insane," Pippa said.

"Suit yourself." I dipped inside, leaving her alone with the shriveled trees and the vultures swaying on the horizon.

After a few minutes, Pippa couldn't stand it anymore. She poked her head through the door, blinking against the dimness. It smelled like rusted metal and old things, like air that hadn't been breathed.

"Trent? If this is your idea of a joke, I'm sure as hell not laughing."

I turned on my flashlight. A halo bounced on the wall. I flicked it on and off like a strobe effect. "Wooo. It's a rave party."

"Stop it," she said. "You're giving me a migraine."

We were in some kind of military hanger. Orange paint flaked off the walls, peeling like a bad sunburn. The ceiling was crisscrossed with aluminum pipes and dangling lamps.

As we staggered forward, I bumped into a traffic cone. I crushed it under my sneaker. The cone fell sideways in front of us. "Get up," I shouted at it. "You can do it. Don't lose hope now."

Pippa was edging toward the door. I turned the flashlight off, leaving us in a blackness so heavy it was almost solid. For a second, I couldn't catch my breath. The dark had knocked it out of me.

"I can see you smiling." I grabbed her waist.

"If you don't let go in two seconds . . ."

I clicked the flashlight on. We both stared at the wall, where a poster of the Statue of Liberty stared back. Her lower half had peeled off, leaving curls of masking tape.

"Don't worry, girl." I tightened my hold around her waist. "You're safe with me."

Pippa jabbed her elbow into my ribs.

I grunted and finally dropped her. "Why the hell did you do that?"

"Because you're being a jerk."

I stood there, rubbing my chest, as if she had inflicted real damage. "We should probably jet. Unless you want to get lung cancer from the asbestos."

"Right," she said, heading straight for the door. Beside the handle was a sign chiseled with faded warnings: *IN CASE*

OF ELECTRIC SHOCK, USE WOODEN POLE OR ROPE TO REMOVE VICTIM.

"Wrong way." I jabbed my thumb in the other direction.

Pippa followed me into the sunlight. I was still thinking about that kiss. This wasn't just any random girl. If I messed up with Pippa, I'd be losing a lot more. Was it worth crossing out of the friend zone? At that moment, I couldn't decide.

"Did you hear that?" she asked.

We listened.

I heard two things: the blood punching into my fingertips and the beat of my sneakers as they sliced through the grass.

"Um. Not really," I said. "Did you take your anti-zombie meds today?"

"Right on schedule." She stuck out her tongue.

"Great. Just what I needed to know."

"Well, you're acting like a complete psycho. Can we go now?"

"Wait up." I thrust an arm in front of her. "Swear to God, I just heard this crazy noise."

"Like what exactly?"

I shrugged. "Couldn't tell you."

"Well, that really makes me feel better."

"Nothing's gonna happen. I've got it all under control. You know. Making the magic happen." I tossed my backpack on the ground and felt around inside. My fingers brushed against metal. The handle almost felt like a toy, but it was real.

"Where did you get that thing?" Pippa asked. "Did you

think we'd be gang-banging in the Everglades? Even rappers couldn't get away with that crap."

"It's my dad's. When I turn twenty-one, I'm getting it registered in my name." I wrapped it in a sweatshirt.

"Please explain why you're carrying a loaded weapon in your backpack."

"It's not loaded."

"And I'm supposed to believe that?"

"Want me to show you?"

She shook her head. "I'll pass."

We walked to the fence, where my army jacket slumped like a dead body. Almost an hour ago, we'd been having fun. Now this entire day had gone to hell.

I crammed my foot in the chain-link and pulled myself over. Pippa took her sweet time, but she made it down first. I was at the top of the fence, trying to yank my jacket from the barbed wire, but it was stuck. I kept tugging until it ripped free.

"That didn't sound good," Pippa said. "Is there a merit badge for sewing? Or maybe you could borrow my Hello Kitty stapler."

"Shut up." I threw the shredded jacket toward the weeds. It cartwheeled in mid-air and landed with a flop. The more I tried not to laugh, the worse it got. Then we both cracked up.

"You're so evil," I said.

Pippa smiled. "I try."

Near the road, a couple of egrets swooped and took off, flapping without a sound. No sign of the Kawasaki.

"It's gotta be somewhere," I muttered.

We pushed back the sawgrass. The jagged leaves stung like a paper cut. I kept looking, though we both knew what I didn't say out loud. The bike was gone.

After what seemed like forever, I finally gave up. I grabbed a rock and pitched it at a stump. "My dad's gonna rip me a new one."

"Let's ask the ranger at the front entrance," Pippa said.

I scanned the horizon, half-expecting the vultures to lift us into the sky. "That's seven miles from here. We're basically screwed. In a couple hours, this place will be so dark even a flashlight won't help."

"Are you serious? What are we supposed to do now?"

"Start walking."

We headed back. Pippa had dragged the camera around all afternoon, yet we'd hardly shot any footage for the so-called Life Portrait documentary. I slid the bag off her shoulder and lifted the camera from its plastic case.

"At least get a light reading first," Pippa muttered.

"It's okay," I said, though I knew she was right. I aimed the lens at her face. The sun was streaming in geometric angles behind her. She was sunburned and sweaty and so amazingly beautiful.

"The focus is off," she said. "You didn't even measure it."

"You're no fun."

"What am I? The entertainment committee?"

"Not even close."

"You're no wilderness man, either. That's pretty obvious. Bet you couldn't even start a fire with a dead twig."

"Out here? Number one, it's too damp. Number two, I'd have the whole tribe on my ass. They've got their own police force and everything."

"So whose side are you on?" she asked.

I lowered my head. I wanted to scream at her, throw stuff, go crazy. Instead, we both stayed quiet. That was the worst part.

Finally, I let her have it. "What a shitty thing to say, Pippa."

"I'm sorry. God. I didn't … I mean, it didn't come out right. That was so wrong. I wasn't trying to put you down."

"Yeah? Well, that's not what it sounded like."

"I'm sorry," she said. "Maybe I should just staple my mouth shut."

"For the record, I'm not about choosing sides."

"I know." Pippa stared at the ground. "I've got something to tell you."

"Okay." Here it comes.

"I see two people in front of me," she said, "and I don't know which is real. When we started hanging out again, I thought you were really cool. I mean, you didn't judge me or anything. Now it feels like you've changed. Like you're afraid of getting close to people. Or you think you're not good enough."

"It sucks that you see me like that."

"True. But guess what? You're more than good enough," she said, and for a moment, I almost believed it.

nine

Me and Pippa sat on this decrepit bench near the ranger station, waiting for a human to show up. I wanted to kiss her again, but she wouldn't even look at me. One minute, she's all into it. The next minute, she's acting like it never happened. I had no clue what was in her brain.

"Maybe we should call your dad," she said.

I tried messing with my cell. No signal. Anyway, I didn't plan on talking to Dad. He was the last person I wanted to deal with.

The shack was locked. I squinted through the window. On the desk, somebody had left a mug full of pencils, a Sudoku Magic puzzle, and a cigar smushed in a skull-shaped ashtray.

"Don't stress," I told Pippa. "He's coming back. Trust me."

We waited. I could only hope it was a ranger who'd dragged the bike off.

He finally materialized a half hour later. He was a little dude, sweat stains circling his arms, and he looked pissed.

"You guys have some explaining to do," he said. It sounded like 'splaining.

I slid off the bench. "Why?"

"Because there's been a theft on the property and we have reason to believe you're involved."

"Right. Somebody stole my bike."

The ranger craned his neck, glaring up at me. "You're Trent Osceola?"

"Aye, captain."

"Your father called Flamingo," he said, meaning the park's main entrance. "Figured you'd be out here. Told us to keep an eye peeled."

"Whatever," I said. "Give me the bike and we'll go."

"He's at the front office."

"He is?"

Dad wasn't supposed to drive. Did he take the Yeti? Of course he did. No doubt he was drunk off his ass. That's for sure. I glanced over at Pippa. She was scraping at her thumbnail, stripping off flakes of glittery black polish.

"You better come with me," the ranger said.

I didn't argue.

———

He drove us to the office in his stupid SUV, the bumper plastered with *Go Green!* bumper stickers. So much for Mother Earth. When he spotted Pippa's camera tucked between her feet, he went ballistic.

"Did you guys take movies inside the park?"

Pippa tried to nudge the camera deeper under the seat. "We only shot one roll."

"No filming without a permit," he said in this dead monotone, like he was hypnotized. He thumped the dashboard. "Don't you know it's against the law?"

"We didn't know."

"Well, that doesn't make it okay. Does it?"

He actually waited for an answer.

"Does it?"

"No," Pippa said in a small voice.

I wanted to smash the guy's teeth out. All thirty-two of them.

My dad was waiting for us, hunched in a metal chair, the kind that wreak havoc on your joints no matter which way you sit. Just looking at his face, I could tell he was wasted.

"This is how you treat your old man?" he said. "You go and pull a fucked-up stunt like this?"

I got a whiff of beer as he stumbled out of the chair. "Let's talk about it later, okay?"

"You're not running the show around here, boy. We'll talk when I damn well please." I'd seen him out of control, but never like this.

We had to sit there, listening to this garbage, while the rangers filled out their stupid papers. When they finally let us go, Dad marched to the Jeep at full speed. There was no stopping him.

"Come on, Dad," I said. "Pass the keys. I'm driving."

"The hell you are."

"Seriously. Let me have the keys."

He opened the door. "You," he said. "Get in."

Pippa scrambled into the back. I couldn't guess what she was thinking.

Actually, I could.

On the ride home, she didn't say one word. Dad was blabbing so much, nobody had a chance. He'd hitched the Kawasaki to the rack, hopped into the driver's seat, and gunned it down the road.

We swerved onto the highway, cutting off a minivan. When the guy behind us honked, Dad rolled down the window and flipped him off. I half-expected bullets to start flying. Road rage or whatever. The guy blasted his horn again: a thin, watery note that lost an octave the farther we raced ahead.

"Don't even start," Dad muttered.

Was he venting at me or the pissed-off driver?

Dad switched back to his favorite subject: no-good sons. He jerked the wheel and pulled into the next lane. Billboards whizzed past, screaming shit about legal fireworks and gator meat.

"Watch it," I said, twisting around to check on Pippa in the backseat. It killed me just imagining how she must feel. Her face was against the glass, her neck wet with tears.

Dad punched the breaks and I slammed into the dashboard. I shifted my gaze to the road. All the trees beside the canal looked scorched, as if lightning had struck them one by one.

We turned the corner for the Rez. In the dark, our neighbor's chickee hut reminded me of a monster, the kind that scared me as a kid staying up and watching late-night horror movies on TV. Then I got a little bigger and wondered what the hell was so scary in the first place.

As we rattled over the driveway, Dad chugged the rest of his Big Gulp. He pitched the cup out the window.

I knew what came next. This is when Angry Dad morphed into Pathetic Dad. If I waited long enough, he'd be sobbing on the couch. Eventually, the sobs faded into snores. The next morning, the stuttery noise of the blender would drill through the house. I'd find him in the garage, pumping iron like nothing ever happened.

Dad wasn't crying now. He got out of the car, marched to the opposite side, and flung open the passenger door. Before I could pry him off, he dragged me onto the pavement. I skidded on my knees, tasted dirt and blood.

"So what's the deal?" he said, lurching toward the Jeep. "This your girlfriend?"

I lifted my head. "Leave her alone."

Dad tugged the handle, but Pippa must've locked it. He pounded on the window. "Hey missy. It's time you got a few things straight," he said, trying the door again. "My son? See, he's screwing this little cha-cha."

"Shut up, Dad. Nobody wants to hear it."

"Comes and goes whenever he likes. Sleeps all day. Leaves a mess all over the house. He's even got the balls to steal my beer. So tell me, missy. Do I look like a fool to you?"

"That's enough. I said shut up. You're drunk."

He spun around. "Don't you ever talk to me like that."

Dad swung his fist. White heat tunneled through my ribs. I rolled face-down in the grass, tried to shield myself with my arms. Kicks came from all directions. No muscle that didn't burn. Even the space inside was swollen.

I squeezed my eyes open. Headlights raked the backyard. In the driveway, there was the Jeep, a hulking metal thing. Pippa watched from the front seat. Her silent face floated behind the windshield.

Dad's voice dissolved into static. It was true, what he said. Pippa deserved better. I was an idiot to think she'd care.

My backpack was on the ground, just a few feet away. It must've fallen when he pulled me from the car. If I could reach it, the gun wouldn't be hard to dig out.

"You got a smart mouth," Dad was saying, "and it's doing you no good. You better sharpen up quick. Because you're no different than me, boy. Your hear that? No different."

Me and Dad? We had nothing in common. He was an asshole who wrote bad checks and cheated on my mom, a freak who couldn't handle a job that required a bigger mental capacity than mowing lawns, a middle-aged loser who got wasted every night just because he couldn't face the sad reality of his non-existence.

It was just fate and genetics that tied us together. That's all.

Light slid across the grass. Uncle Seth walked out of his house. He was usually in there watching game shows with his girlfriend.

"Get up," Dad told me. "Stand like a man."

I didn't move.

"Everything okay?" Uncle Seth called out.

"This ain't your business. Got that? It's between me and him."

Uncle Seth flicked his gaze in my direction. "Why don't you head inside and we'll talk it out?"

"You heard what I said."

Dad turned and I made a lunge for the backpack. I tightened my grip around the strap and hauled it closer. My hands shook as I yanked the zipper, felt the gun's plastic handle wrapped in my sweatshirt. I didn't plan on doing anything stupid. Like I told Pippa, it wasn't loaded. I just wanted to scare the shit out of him.

The .357 Mag fit in my palm like it was meant to be there. I looped my finger around the trigger—a major rule-breaker, unless you meant to blow somebody away. Got up on my feet. Stood like a man. Exactly what Dad had told me to do.

When he saw the gun, his expression shifted. "Give me that thing. Shit. You don't even know how to operate it."

"Yeah? You want proof?"

Man, it felt good telling him off. And I wasn't done yet. There was a lot Dad needed to hear. Unfortunately, I didn't get the chance.

He clamped onto my arm, wrenching so tight I groaned. We staggered around the yard. I shoved all my weight into him. He wobbled against me, crushing down on my shoulder.

But he was still drunk, and I was the stronger one. I knew that now.

An explosion of noise rocked through my fist. I was so freaked out I tossed the gun. It skittered across the driveway. The smell of metal sharpened the air. My ears were ringing and I'd forgotten how to breathe.

I gawked at the Mag, the way it glinted on the pavement. Why the hell was it loaded? Dad was always grilling me on the Ten Commandments of Fire Arms Safety. Rule *numero uno*: Keep nothing in the chamber.

Smoke draped the trees like gauze. I stood there, breathing in slow-motion, trying to decide what to do. If Dad caught me moving toward the gun, he'd see where it had landed and grab it first. I thought about Pippa, trapped in the car. No way could I ditch her. She was the one shining thing in the void I called my life.

I had to choose.

Stay or go.

I was stuck on pause, unable to move or make a decision, until a siren tugged me back to consciousness. It sounded so fake—a TV sound effect. A pair of spinning halos swooped over the house, shifting back and forth, red to blue. I squinted in the brightness.

Then I ran.

ten

Houses zoomed past me, one after another, all facing north. Each came with a chickee hut, a satellite dish, and at least two SUVs—the basic necessities of life. Everybody on the Rez planted little backyard gardens for the Green Corn Dance in summer. You're supposed to plant the seed and take care of it. There's a big celebration, lots of dancing and singing, and the boys get new names.

It was all about letting go of mistakes and starting over again.

This was supposed to be my home, but I didn't have a freaking clue where to go. I hadn't done much exploring since moving to the Rez. It was just another neighborhood, twenty miles outside Miami.

Why was I running like a criminal? My dad was the one who'd fucked up. You could say he'd made a career out of it. Now I was dealing with his garbage on top of everything else, as if I needed an excuse to hate myself. That was the easy part.

I ran until my lungs burned. When I couldn't gulp another breath, I doubled over and puked in the grass. The sickness came in waves. At first I'd think it was done, then my stomach made other plans.

As I wiped my mouth, I glanced at the concrete valley surrounding me. Somehow I'd landed in a skate park. Who knew the Rez had an awesome spot like this? Man, if I'd lived here as a kid, I'd have been skating here every damn minute, popping ollies off those sweet-looking ramps. Maybe I'd actually have mastered the art of kickflipping. I wasn't learning any new tricks now. I was seventeen. In other words, old.

Seventeen used to sound light-years away. What would I be doing then? Touring the world and partying with my band in true rock-star fashion? I didn't have a band. I hardly picked up my Gibson. It was scratched to hell. The E string was busted and I needed a new amp. Of course, Dad had promised to get this stuff for me. Like most of his endless promises, it never happened.

I walked up the half-pipe and crouched at the top, dangling my feet over the edge. My ribs ached. All of a sudden, I was sweating like crazy. It felt like I was suffocating. I unlaced my sneakers and peeled them off. Tossed them in a pile next to a Red Bull can that somebody had crushed on the pavement.

The street lamp clicked on and off, as if it couldn't decide what to do: light up the peach-colored concrete, or fold the park in a darkness so thick it almost had a taste. I sat there, feeling sorry for myself. Thinking about Pippa, telling her all kinds of embarrassing shit I'd never say out loud. Take sex, for example. I should've waited instead of rushing into it. At the time, it was just something to get over with. No use lying.

Would she ever talk to me again?

Everybody at school used to make fun of us. They called her my girlfriend back in fifth grade. Whatever. They were idiots. And it's weird because I wouldn't even touch her whenever we said goodbye. It became this big joke. She'd grab me and I'd back away, fake coughing like her hugs were a cloud of Black Death.

Right now, there was nothing I wanted more.

I needed to hold her so bad.

In my mind, I was screaming. I couldn't go back to the house. But I felt like a coward for leaving her there, alone with Dad and the cops. They probably arrested his drunk ass. Where was I supposed to go now? Maybe I could hunt down my grandma's number in Fort Myers. Yeah right. The patron saint of greyhounds—I was so unworthy of her time. She sent cards every Christmas, along with 8x10 glossies of her fur babies.

Who was I kidding? I mean, honestly. Why would Pippa want to be with me? She was this amazing girl with all kinds of stuff going on. Not to mention the cutest smile ever.

If Pippa knew the crap I thought about, she'd bolt in the other direction, like I was a zombie or something. I'd eat her brains out. That's what I'd do. If you stayed with me long enough, this is what happened. The world turned to ashes like in my favorite video game, *Silent Hill*. Even Pyramid Head, the ultimate bad guy, didn't stand a chance against it.

I destroyed everything I touched.

That's all I could think about, contemplating the evil nature of my universe from that damn half-pipe. Then a bunch of skaters showed up—little badasses, all thugged out in their gold chains and tie-dyed shirts. They were taking turns slurping a gallon-sized jug of iced tea and spitting it at each other. This skinny kid with a mouthful of metal was laughing hardcore. I couldn't remember when I'd laughed like that.

"Nice hat." He saluted me.

I returned the salute. "Thanks."

"You got a big cut on your face," he said.

I got the feeling he wasn't judging me. Just stating the obvious, the way twelve-year-olds do. "Yeah," I told him. "That's what I figured."

"Does it hurt?" he asked.

"Only when I smile."

He nodded as if this made perfect sense. "Try not to smile, then."

"Good advice."

The others stayed back. They were blabbing in that slippery language, Hitchiti, the tribe's native tongue. Except it didn't really belong to us. It was a mix of Creek and Choctaw. That much I'd learned from Wikipedia. My uncle only spoke Hitchiti in front of tourists.

The skinny kid rolled off with his buddies. One of them glanced over his shoulder and said a word that made me sick all over again: "*Hatki*."

White.

He actually thought I was white.

This was fucked up on so many levels. I mean, yeah. My mom was from the UK. "Across the pond" was how she put it. Not that you'd ever guess by looking at my skin, the same color as maple syrup. Sometimes people would talk Spanish at me. God, that really pissed me off. They just assumed I knew what the hell they were saying. They never asked.

While the Miccosukee kids did their thing, I wished I could zoom into another dimension. I'd tell them it doesn't get better. All that shit about "doing your best" in school and making good grades in Geometry. What does it get you? A stupid desk job in an office.

I'd tell them to live every second like the last. Not the most original statement. Still, it's better than the crap you get in school. My teachers couldn't even admit that Columbus didn't "discover" America. It was there from the start.

Why doesn't somebody tell the truth? Nothing gets better unless you make it happen. There should be a special class. Call it Reality 101. You could learn about stuff that really matters. Like what to do if your dad gets wasted and decides to use you as a punching bag.

The Miccosukee kids looked so free, gliding back and forth on the ramps. When they crashed, it was no big deal. They just got back up again. My new friend, Mr. Skinny, tried to kickflip onto a ramp. Of course, he was doing it all wrong.

After watching him eat pavement like a million times, I finally said, "Hey newb. Let me see that board."

He circled around the rails, then slowed in front of me. "Why? You want to steal it?"

"Nah. I've seen better boards at Kmart."

"Oh, so you're an expert?" he said, stepping off it. "That's why your face is wrecked? You tried to vert and got a concussion?"

I shrugged. "The wack meter doesn't lie."

Mr. Skinny was amped now. "Well, I'd like to see you throw down."

"Sure," I said. "Prepare to be owned."

He shoved the board at me. "How about those rails?" he said, walking toward the opposite end of the park.

I'd never grinded on a rail. That trick was impossible to pull off. You couldn't even practice it. Not without multiple levels of hell. Man, what did I get myself into?

This was going to suck.

As I stepped onto the board, he yelled, "Dude. What happened to your shoes?"

"Don't need them."

His buds rolled to the side. They held out their cell phones, ready to snap a picture, waiting for me to fail.

I steered toward the cement pyramid. It felt good to skate again. I'd forgotten how much it chilled my brain. All the shit that happened today.

When I picked up enough speed, I ollied onto the rail. As I locked my back wheels against the metal edge, I stayed centered. The pain inside my muscles dripped away. I wasn't thinking about anything. I got caught between the cement and the sky. I was right there, floating in that space outside the "now."

I was exactly where I needed to be.

I slid for a couple seconds, then bailed. The kids came running up to me, yelling all kinds of nonsense. I only heard bits and pieces. Guess I was still in the nowhere zone, not functioning on a human level yet.

"That was a high-ass ollie. Seriously, man. I can't believe you did it barefoot. That was sick," said Mr. Skinny, pounding my shoulder. "What clan are you?"

"Panther," I said.

This was sort of a lie.

I was clanless.

"You know my Uncle Seth?" I asked.

"Yeah. But I've never seen you before. You go to school here?"

I kicked the board to him. "Nah, I'm at Palm Hammock."

He chewed the end of his gold chain. "Isn't that, like, in Kendall or something?"

The others stayed quiet. They were trying to size me up. That much was obvious. Did I belong here on the Rez? Or was I better off in the suburbs, like the white kids and the Cubans?

"You're Trent. That's your name, right?" said another kid. He kept popping his retainer, sliding it out with his tongue. Man, I'm glad I never got braces. "Your uncle does the gator show 'cause they got rid of Manny."

Who the hell was Manny? It seemed like everybody knew

each other on the Rez, like we were one big family. But I wasn't from here. I'd come onto the scene too late. Now it felt like I'd never catch up.

"Yeah, that's Uncle Seth. The Alligator Man," I said and they laughed. Sometimes it's too easy, getting kids to laugh. They hopped on their boards and rolled off.

I wanted to trade places with those kids. Seriously. What did they have to worry about? They grew up with PlayStations and cable TV. But they could probably steer an airboat, one-handed, across the Glades. Soon they'd become men with new names.

Yeah. The Miccosukee kids had it good.

It started pouring. Cold, stabbing drops speckled the cement. I leaned back and stuck out my tongue, catching the flavorless rain. No doubt it was laced with chemicals from all the junk people chucked in our lakes. The clouds sucked it up and dumped it on us. That's the way things worked. If you put something out there, it always swung around to you.

The skaters were doing tricks in the rain—pulling off back-side 180s and landing killer pop shove-its. Then they stopped all at once, as if somebody hit pause on a video game. Mr. Skinny and his buds huddled behind me, clutching their boards.

"Oh shit," he said.

The light bounced around the park, flickering off the ramps and grind rails.

"Which one of you is Trent?" somebody called out. He stood near the trees—a cop waving a flashlight.

All the kids gawked at their feet. Still, they didn't rat me out. I give them props for that.

"Don't waste my time," he told us.

"It's me," I blurted, hating the sound of my voice, the way it cracked.

"Thank you," he said, as if I'd done him a favor. "The rest of you guys need to leave."

They scattered. No time wasted.

"Okay Trent." The cop turned to me. "What's the story?"

"Chilling."

"Well, you can't chill here. Come over and sit down a second."

God, this was so freaking stupid. My dad was the one in trouble. Why was I getting hassled? Sure, I'd messed up. But that didn't make me a bad person.

I squatted on the sidewalk like a fugitive.

"All right, Trent. Let's talk, okay? Here's the deal. Your father says you got into some sort of altercation and ran off. You want to tell me what's going on?"

How could I shape it into words? My dad got wasted. That's the way it goes. The man drinks a sixer every night. This time, he got a little out of control. He didn't mean to hit me. It just happened.

"Me and my dad started fighting," I told the cop.

"Okay," he said. It seemed like "okay" was his default answer for everything. "Can you tell me what happened?"

"He got mad."

"Any idea why?"

"Because I took something."

"You mean something that wasn't yours."

I focused on the dent above his lip. If you stared at one part of somebody's face, you didn't have to look them in the eye. That's a little trick I've learned.

"Answer me." He was totally over it now. "Did you steal your father's motorcycle?"

"Sort of," I mumbled.

"Well, is it true or not?"

"Listen. I already told you—" I started to get up, but he pushed me, dropping a hand on my shoulder. I could've sued for harassment.

The cop had no off button. He kept blasting away, screaming shit like, "When I talk, you listen."

Why did I have to listen? It's not like anybody listened to me. Just because he had a badge and gun didn't mean the universe put him in charge. Just thinking about guns made my stomach twist. If I got blamed for messing with it, they could charge me with illegal possession of a firearm. Then what would happen? I'd go straight to jail. That's what.

"Just stay where you're at. You got yourself a whole world of trouble. Do you want to make it worse?"

So typical. Why did cops always ask dumb questions like "Do you want to make it worse?" I mean, come on. Did he really expect an answer? This night couldn't get any worse. You could pretty much bank on it.

The cop was getting soaked. I could tell he was totally over this situation. He told me to follow him to the car, which was parked behind a building with coral rock walls. This was the school those kids mentioned. More than anything, I wanted to zap myself into their reality. Start over. Get a new name, one that belonged to me.

I'd never been arrested before. Was he going to slap on the handcuffs? He still hadn't mentioned the gun. Somebody must've heard it go off. Wouldn't be the first time.

"Am I going to jail?" Might as well face the truth.

He studied my face. "Just calm down, okay? Your cheek looks a little swollen. How did that happen?"

If I stuck to the facts, he'd probably throw Dad's ass behind bars. Then I'd get sent to juvie or whatever. "I was skating, right? And I fell." That's what I told him.

"Where's your board?"

"Back there with my sneakers." Another lie, but how would he know?

"So the rest of your stuff is in the park. Is that it?"

"Yeah."

"What are you doing, running around with no shoes? You could step on broken glass. There's scorpions out here, too. Saw a big one yesterday. Almost gave me a heart attack."

"Please," I said. "Just tell me if I'm going to jail."

He slammed the door so hard I flinched. "Jail? That's where you want to go?"

Again. Another dumb question.

"No sir."

The "sir" probably tripped him up. He stared. "Trent, I'm taking you home."

"What?" I must've blanked out or something. A high-pitched noise stung my eardrum. Damaged nerves. I don't know.

The cop pressed his fat arms on the window. "How old are you?"

I couldn't think straight. "Eighteen. No. I mean, I'll be eighteen this summer."

He nodded. "Okay. Sit tight."

"Maybe you could drop me off someplace?" I was almost begging.

"I'm not a taxi," he said, walking away, slow as hell.

I shivered against the fake leather seat, thinking about all the bad guys who'd sat in this same spot—the men who hurt people and took things away. I wanted to bust out of there. Just breathing in that stale, air-conditioned car made me feel dirty.

"Can I go back and get my stuff?"

"Listen, kid. I'm giving you a break here." He got behind the wheel and started messing with a laptop—a clunky old Dell mounted to the seat. My school had better computers than that piece of crap.

"I just want my hat," I whispered.

"Unbelievable." He punched a couple keys on the laptop. Glanced at me again. "Do you smart-mouth your father like that?"

"You don't know shit about my dad." I turned away from him, twisting my body as far as possible.

He got so quiet, I could hear the laptop's empty hum. "Something you want to tell me? Go on. Now's your chance."

This guy couldn't make up his mind. Talk. Don't talk. Well, I wasn't talking to a cop. That's for damn sure.

"Okay," he said. "It's your choice. Totally up to you."

That was a complete lie.

Nothing was up to me. I had no control unless I detached from reality. That's how skating used to feel if I landed a sweet trick. The same numbing effect when I blasted tunes on my Gibson. Or when I finally unlocked Prestige Mode on Call of Duty. And when I was flying down the highway with Pippa. All the beatings in the world couldn't make me trade that moment in time.

As the car lurched through the neighborhood, I kept my eyes shut. I didn't need to see the road. I could sense every turn, all the stops and starts.

I wasn't going anywhere.

eleven

Headlights scraped away the darkness. As we pulled up to the house, I glanced through the window and there was Pippa in the yard. She looked so worn out, like a smaller, less intense version of herself.

The cop marched me to the front door where my dad stood, waiting. I tried to move toward Pippa, but Dad got in the way.

"They got into another one of their crazy fights." He wouldn't shut up. "Teenagers, right?"

"That's bullshit and you know it," I said.

"Just settle down, okay?" the cop told me. "You're in enough trouble right now."

I watched the man's face, the way it changed. If I told the truth, would he believe me? Or would it make things worse? Maybe I would go to jail. And if that didn't happen, Dad would knock me around again. In my head, I got this picture: me and Pippa in the backyard, playing pirates, the rope tightened around us.

"That's the girlfriend." Dad jerked his thumb at Pippa. If I could've jumped on him, I would've ripped his lips off. But I couldn't breathe, much less jump.

"Is that true?" the cop asked.

I glanced at Pippa, but she kept her head down. Behind her, a macramé plant hanger dangled. It looked like something a kid would make in art class. It tilted in the damp breeze, tipped and swayed in pointless circles.

"Yes," I said.

"Yes what?"

"She's my girlfriend."

He nodded like he knew all along. "Okay then. Thanks for being honest."

Ten minutes later, the cop was leading Pippa to the car and pushing her into the backseat like a criminal. I stood there feeling helpless as they passed the mailbox at the end of our street—a metal box strapped to a giant paperclip-looking thing, defying gravity and logic. I couldn't stop thinking about Pippa, who was sitting where I'd been just minutes before.

My mind shuffled through a montage, as Mr. Bones would call it: Pippa kissing me inside the abandoned missile base. The weight of the motorcycle rumbling beneath us. Her skin, warm against mine.

I wanted zombie powers more than ever. I'd run straight to Pippa's window and carry her to the Everglades. We'd learn the secrets that only gators know: the stillness of things, waiting for just the right moment, as we sank beneath the surface.

There were no trees at the end of my block. Only a canal

laced with weeds. I didn't have magical powers. I couldn't even shape my thoughts into words. The cop had done all the talking. He'd told Dad that I was walking a fine line. He'd seen it before. And I better stay away from girls if I knew what was good for me. But there was something he didn't understand.

Pippa was good for me.

———

The day after the "incident," Dad went back to his usual bullshit. He didn't apologize for freaking out. He didn't talk about what happened. He just revved up the blender and gulped his stupid protein shakes.

I stayed out of his way, as much as possible.

In my cave, I read magazines about black holes and the mysterious force known as dark energy. I didn't want to go back to school, but compared to sitting around the house, it was starting to look semi-endurable. Plus, I was missing Pippa like crazy. I tried calling her cell a million times, but it always went straight to voicemail. Either she hadn't paid her crackberry bill or she was completely ignoring me.

Could I really blame Pippa for cutting me off? She must've been scared out of her mind. I doubt that she'd ever seen shit like that. Unfortunately, it was becoming part of my daily existence.

By afternoon, Dad was acting nice again. He was all like, "Let's get some new tires for the Jeep." And "How does pizza sound for dinner?" It was totally bizarre. So I'd just nod at him or slide my way out.

Meanwhile, a bruise had leaked across my cheekbone, like somebody attacked me with a Sharpie. My ribs still throbbed whenever I coughed. Worst of all, there was the shame of what Dad did to me.

Dark energy.

That's what I was made of.

I stared at the marks on my body and planned my revenge. First, I'd slam my fist into his teeth. Then I'd pound him so hard, he'd need his jaw wired shut. That way I wouldn't have to hear his stupid lies anymore.

On Monday morning, I crashed so hard I didn't wake up in time for class. Okay. That's an understatement. I stayed passed out until late afternoon. My spirit was definitely in the land of the dead. When I woke up, I heard Dad yelling on the phone.

"Who's in charge of that school?" he yelled. "A pack of morons?"

At least that's something we could agree on.

It didn't take long to figure it out—I'd gotten suspended for skipping. So the school was like, "Trent's failing all his classes," then they tell me to stay home. Yeah, that made a lot of sense.

Here's the equation:

Avoiding Dad + School Suspension = 0

I grabbed the keys to the Yeti. Fast-walked through the living room. Dad had finally stopped yelling. I listened for his boomy voice. Hard to believe he used to sing in a band. His vocal cords were shot to hell. Yeah. Mr. Rock Star. Living the dream.

Dad was standing near the kitchen window. He must've felt my stare, the laser beam of hate pouring into his neck. "Think you're special? Is that what your mother told you? That's why she put you in that special school, huh? A music school. What a fucking joke."

He moved in my direction. Until right then, I hadn't even looked at him. I was way too freaked out. His massive gut swelled above his shorts. Tattoos stained his bare legs. He was bigger than me in a way that had nothing to do with strength.

We were right there, both of us.

"Where's your special school now?" he went on. "You can't even hack it in that school for idiots. So what does that make you?"

"I'm not an idiot."

"You sure about that? Because I used to be like you. A hot shot. Up on stage, thinking I was in the big leagues. Only an idiot would believe that. Keep dreaming, son. You're never gonna be anything."

Dad left the kitchen. He didn't even try to stop me from taking off. It was pretty obvious he didn't care. I bet he wanted me to go away permanently. Crash my car on the Florida Turnpike and die in a flaming wreck. Yeah, he would probably enjoy that.

I reached for a glass on the table, but it was dirty. Same with the cups in the sink. I leaned over the counter and turned on the faucet. Stuck my head under the cold water. Gulped it down until my throat turned numb.

———

The sun was fading as I cruised through my old neighborhood. Pippa's house was on the corner near the canal. As I sped past, I couldn't help imagining her there on the porch, looking real cute in her checkered tights.

I was smiling so hard, my cheeks stung. The smile melted when I reached the house-formerly-known-as-mine. That big-ass Ford was parked crookedly in the driveway. My mom's boyfriend. She'd been seeing him off and on for a while, but I could never remember his name.

Mr. Nameless waddled into the backyard. He had these camo shorts that looked diaperish, a stupid pair of wrap-around sunglasses, and a jug of bleach. I watched him crouch on the lawn like a garden gnome.

God, I hated him.

He was slopping bleach all over the place, making a giant mess. This was his cheap attempt at killing weeds. What's so bad about weeds, anyway? You can make wishes on dandelions. Nobody ever wished on a carnation, as far as I can tell.

I pulled down the sun visor and leaned back, just in case he saw me. As I rolled past, Mom slipped out of the garage. She was chugging from a tall plastic cup, but I figured it was her beverage of choice: white wine. Nice job, Mom. Nothing like getting the party started before sundown.

That's one thing she had in common with Dad.

Maybe the only thing.

She squinted up at the car. I'm sure she recognized the Yeti. After all, it used to be hers back in the day. And don't get me wrong. I was mad as hell. But when her eyes locked onto mine, I got this weird tingle in the back of my throat. I mean, she's still my mom, right?

For a second, I almost pulled over. Would she let me stay if I promised not to damage her life? Maybe things could go back to normal. Yeah, I must've been crazy thinking shit like that. As long as Mr. Nameless was in charge, nothing would ever be normal.

Then I noticed the *For Sale* sign.

It was lassoed with party balloons, like it might lift into the sky. I kept staring at it, hoping the sign would do just that. I could totally picture it—the grass unrolling like a carpet, tugging my mom, Mr. Nameless, and everything else along with it.

My stream-of-consciousness went like this:

Am I being punked?

Mom is NOT selling the house.

She just can't.

I slammed the brakes. Turned off the ignition. Jumped out and marched over to He Who Shall Remain Nameless. The sting of bleach cut the air. My vision blurred as I got closer. He acted all surprised and stuck out his hand, offering me a fist-bump, which, of course, I ignored.

"Trenton," he said, as if my name was a greeting on another planet.

Did I mention that I hated him?

Mom tugged me into a hug. She still hadn't let go of her drink. The cold plastic cup seared into my ribs.

"What happened to your eye?" Mom was staring. Big time.

"Nothing."

She grabbed hold of my chin and twisted it against the sunlight. Mom's death-grip was brutal. She used to lick her thumb and smear the dirt off my face. I almost expected her to do it again. But even Mom's spit couldn't erase the stain under my skin.

I pointed at the *For Sale* sign. "You're selling the house?"

Mom chewed her lip. I knew what that meant.

It meant she was going to start lying.

"Well, I've been meaning to talk to you, love," she said, taking another sip of her drink. She chomped the ice and didn't say anything else.

Mr. Nameless took over. "This place is too big for us. We could save a lot of money not having to pay property taxes."

Us.

We.

Not me.

I grabbed the cup out of Mom's hand and slam-dunked it. Ice cubes skittered across the driveway, leaving snail trails in the sun. "You didn't even tell me!" I was screaming now. "I can't believe you're doing this!"

"Stop it," Mom said. "You're getting all worked up. My god. It's only a house."

"Oh right. I forgot. I'm not allowed to express an opinion."

"Look at you, all cheesed off about nothing." The more booze she guzzled, the more British she sounded. "My god, Trent. It's not like I'm abandoning you."

"Too late for that," I said, walking away.

A hand sank onto my shoulder.

"Trenton."

I spun around, completely on auto pilot. Balled up my fist, reeled back, and swung.

Mr. Nameless didn't see it coming.

Neither did I.

In my entire life, I'd never hit another human being. Guess there's a first time for everything. He sort of tripped sideways, flinging his arms out. I give him credit, though. Five seconds later, he staggered back on his feet like Stone Cold Steve.

Mom was freaking. "What's wrong with you?" she kept yelling. Basically letting me know I was going to hell. When I reached the car, she said, "You're no better than your father."

It killed me, hearing her say that.

A rope had knotted up inside me. I could feel it getting stronger, pulling at my guts, as I struggled to break free.

I shoved the key in the ignition. The Yeti lurched forward and slammed to a stop. I tried a couple more times. Same deal. I jiggled the clutch and finally gunned it out of the driveway. So much for my dramatic exit.

As I drove, my head was looping on double speed. I'd been roaming without a destination all day. I couldn't go back to the Rez because Dad was there. And wherever he was, you wouldn't find me. At this point, we were opposing forces of nature.

I slowed for a red light and grabbed my cell. Out of habit, I started scrolling through my non-deleted emails. I pressed the phone against my ear, soaked up another dose of radiation while it hum-hum-hummed the audio equivalent of a blank stare. I couldn't stop thinking about rockets and skating barefoot in the rain, the memory of Pippa, the taste of her mouth.

My finger slid over Pippa's number as if pulled by a Death Star tractor beam. No hello, no voicemail, no luck. What was the deal with this girl? Yeah, I could've texted her or whatever. Forget it. My humiliation had reached full capacity.

I glanced at my inbox. Enough spamwiches to feed a World War II platoon.

Subject: Sexy Russian Girls Looking For Please You
Sender: oksana@bonbon.net

Delete.

Subject: Considering an Exciting New Career in the Culinary Arts?
Sender: admissions@LeCroutonAcademy.edu

Delete.

Subject: FWD: Send to 6 people in 6 minutes
and receive 6 good luck blessings. This is scary!
The phone will ring after you do this!
Sender: bonsaikitten@aol.com

Delete.

Subject: You Suck
Sender: AlvaroTheGMan@hotmail.com
...

That's all he wrote. Just a row of dot-dot-dots. What
kind of message was that? Morse Code?

I pulled over. Dialed up the G Man. A blast of techno
wreaked havoc on my eardrums while I waited for him to pick
up.

"Yo Trent," he said. "*Que lo que*? Did you get hit by a car
this weekend? Because that's the only excuse I'm willing to tol-
erate. I mean, seriously."

"Sorry I missed your set. How was it?" I asked.

"Epic. This crazy girl was dancing on stage, right? And she
fell and they had to carry her out on a stretcher."

"Sounds pretty epic."

"Michelle was there," he added.

"She was?"

"Yeah," he said. "What's the status on that?"

I hesitated for a second. "We're done."

"For real? Man, how could you let that go?"

There was no point in explaining. Meanwhile, Alvaro was
going on about my ex. Or (as he put it), *DJ Hotness to the
Extreme*.

"Is it okay if I call her?" he wanted to know.

Wasn't there an unspoken rule? *Thou shalt not date thy friend's ex.*

"Why? You plan on trading mixtapes? I think she's already got *The Ultimate 80s Pool Party.*"

"So, what are you doing now?" he asked, totally ignoring my sarcasm.

I could've told him the truth: I'm sitting in a parking lot under the I-95 overpass, trying to hide from my dad. And today I learned that I'm an idiot. That's one of the many life lessons Dad has taught me.

"I'm driving around, wasting gas," I said. In other words, stating the obvious.

"Wanna chill at my house? Unless you're too busy having a pow-wow. Is that why you've been missing in action? Smoking too much peyote?"

I knew he was just busting my balls. This was Alvaro. Pure ridiculousness. But it pissed me off, hearing him say that. Usually I would've laughed. Instead, I hung up. Then I felt stupid. All that stuff about peyote and pow-wows.

Here's the part that really sucked.

I let him get away with it.

twelve

Dozens of cars lined the block. It looked like every relevant person from my old school, as well as a ton I didn't recognize, had showed up at Alvaro's place. This wasn't exactly my definition of "chilling."

The front window glowed with one of those creepy religious candles. Above the words *Pray for Us*, a heart floated in a nest of fire. When I looked at it, I couldn't help thinking about my own heart, thudding under my ribs.

Music throbbed behind the door. I pushed my way inside. A crowd of intense-looking people were attempting to dance in the living room. They kept bumping into the furniture, the wall, and each other. I scooted around them and headed straight for the kitchen, the safest place. Or so I thought.

"Hey, Mr. Pow-Wow."

Somebody chucked a handful of ice at my face. The stinging cold made me wince. Alvaro was sitting on the counter, swinging his legs in circles. He reached into the sink and scooped up more half-melted chunks.

"You're looking a little out of it, *tiguere*," he said. "What the hell happened to you?"

"The zombie apocalypse."

"Are you mocking me? Stay still so I can destroy you." He chucked another ice cube, aiming for my head. I ducked. Chips of ice slid down the wall.

Alvaro had it good. His parents were always flying back and forth "on business," whatever that meant. Basically, his grandma was the only living person I ever saw in the house (if "living" means watching Telemundo all day).

"Care for some hooch?" He jiggled a bottle in my face.

"Yeah, sure."

Alvaro ripped into a stack of Dixie cups. "Keeping it classy," he said, dumping beer until it foamed to the rim. "The finest apricot ale from Canada. Because everything's cooler up there."

I took a gulp and cringed at the fruity sweetness. "Think I'll pass."

"You're passing on free beer?" He shrugged. "If it involves alcohol, I'm yessing it. Besides," he said, "I only drink to get drunk. Otherwise, it's like, what's the point?"

Last summer, me and Alvaro used to snatch-and-grab cases of beer from the Bait and Tackle place in Homestead. Then we'd get wasted on the boat docks. It was fun for a while. Why did it seem so stupid now?

Somebody hugged me from behind. I wrestled myself free and there was Michelle, almost unrecognizable in a plaid dress and furry boots. I imagined her rolling logs or whatever lumberjacks were supposed to do.

"Hello Trenton," she said. "Long time no talk."

No talk? We'd never really talked at all.

My beer was tasting a little less odd, the more I drank. "Hmm," I said, draining what was left of it.

Michelle clicked her tongue, like she always did in the middle of a conversation. Not that I'd call it a conversation. When she finally looked at me, she beamed another classic stare in my direction. "What did you say?"

"I didn't say anything. I just made unintelligible noises."

"That's pretty much what I thought. I was just talking to Alvaro," she said, smiling up at him. "And we're having a little debate. Here's the question: If you could have a superpower, what would you pick?"

Question: Why did I ever go out with you?

"I'd pick invisibility," I said, scooting around her.

"Hold on a second." She grabbed my wrist. I couldn't believe she was crossing that line. Actually, I could believe it. "You have to be nice."

"I don't have to be anything."

Alvaro slid off the counter. "I've got a superpower. Can I show you?"

"Shut up, Alvaro. You're confused." Michelle laughed over the music. "Something's wrong with you, like, mentally."

He shoved an ice cube between his teeth. "Yeah? You didn't say that last night."

"That's because you were dreaming." Michelle pulled me

toward the sliding glass door, uber-cool as always. The patio was empty except for a guy smoking weed at a table near the pool.

"You're still here?" she said to the guy as we passed him. She settled into a wicker chair that reminded me of a throne, slung her bare legs over the arm, then motioned for me to do the same. The cushions were flecked with dog hair, which I ignored, although I was a little grossed out.

Michelle rolled her eyes at the weedhead. "I know you're enjoying your little smokefest, but would you mind giving us some privacy?"

"Nah, I was about to snack it up with some fries." The guy licked his palm. "Not just any fries. They've got sea salt. All natural. Just like my girlfriend."

"God, you're so ignorant." Michelle turned to me. "That's my little cousin Juan. He's a pervert. Sorry, but it's true."

"Hell yes. I heard that," Juan said.

"Wow. That's funny. Can you hear this? How about you *vamos*? Now."

Juan pushed himself away from the table but still didn't leave.

"Must ... fight ... chair gravity."

"Do I have to come over there and kick your ass?"

Juan almost tripped, he moved so fast. He was a lot younger than us. I didn't notice that before.

Michelle scrounged inside her purse, took out a lighter and a pack of menthols. "You still don't smoke, do you, Trenton?"

If she already knew, why ask?

Without thinking, I reached for a cigarette.

"Oh nice. A social smoker," Michelle said, flicking her lighter. "Your kind gets no love from me. When it comes to bodily corruption, might as well go all the way." She blew out smoke. "God, why are you not talking? I hope you're not cutting me off. I mean, we can stay close, right?"

She waited for my answer.

This girl cheated on me. It's totally possible that she cheated the whole time we were together. Now my friend is trying to hook up with her. And she wants to "stay close"? What's that supposed to mean?

I pinched the cigarette between my fingers. Even pretending to smoke was too much effort.

Michelle shifted forward in her chair. "So tell me about your new girlfriend. Why isn't she here? I'd really like to meet her."

I slid my eyes to the pool, all lit up with electric stars scattered across the deep end. Alvaro's parents were probably millionaires. The palm trees looped with tiny white lights, the carnivorous-looking orchids that dangled around the table... none of it seemed real.

"I've known Pippa forever," I told her.

"That's so cute. You guys went to school together?"

"We went to childhood together."

"So you guys are like childhood sweethearts?"

Something changed in her tone, which had dropped a hundred degrees south of friendly. All jokes and smiles gone. I was stupid to think she actually wanted to be friends.

I started doodling on my sneaker, decorating the filthy

heel with shooting stars. "Next-door neighbors," I explained. That was the truth. Or it used to be.

"And you slept at each other's houses and everything? That's majorly adorable," she said, touching my arm.

"Every Friday after school. Until her mom shut it down. She didn't want me over anymore. We were 'getting too big for slumber parties.' That's what she told my mom."

I gawked at my jiggling sneaker, all the sloppy constellations that bled into the laces.

Michelle was obviously getting a thrill out of this information. "And then you guys stopped talking? That's so wrong."

"It wasn't like we planned it," I said, stabbing the pen into my shoe. "It just happened."

"Did you guys play kissing games and stuff? I bet you got caught. You know. Show me yours, I'll show you mine..."

I glanced at the sliding glass doors, where Alvaro was throwing ice down a girl's shirt. After all this pointless drama, I thought Michelle would drop the subject.

I thought wrong.

Michelle took out a giant hair clip, the sharp-toothed kind that reminds me of bear traps. She clamped it on her head, leaned forward, and said, "Does she know that you're pretending to be Indian now?"

"What do you mean, 'pretending'?"

She unclipped her hair and tied it back into the same exact shape. "You didn't grow up on the reservation. Are you even allowed to be there? Or are you just crashing at your dad's because your mom got tired of you?"

When she said it, a rush of heat crawled up my neck. "It's really unfair to judge."

"I'm not judging. Honestly. Just trying to help you out."

"You don't really know me, Michelle," I said. "You have no fucking clue what's going on with my life."

"Oh, your friend told me all about it."

"Alvaro told you?" I was starting to feel sick.

"He said you've been missing in action lately. It must be hard for you."

"What's hard?" I asked, falling right into it.

"Living with your dad. I hear he drinks a lot. But I guess that's pretty typical. I mean, where you live."

I slowly got up from the table. Maybe I should've stuck around and defended myself. Or my dad, at least. But it didn't seem worth the effort. Michelle was too busy shredding my soul.

"Maybe that's why this girl stopped talking to you," she said. "Your family situation is just too ... different."

When I reached the sliding glass door, I yanked, but it wouldn't budge. On the other side was Alvaro, laughing his stupid head off. I pounded on the glass until he finally let me inside.

"Yo. Mr. Pow-Wow." Alvaro was up in my space, making a big deal about blocking the way out.

I pushed him. Hard. He stumbled backward, sloshing his beer. Half of it soaked my shirt.

"Whoa there. No reason to get violent," he said.

Everybody was acting like this was ultra hilarious. I was a

joke to them. My life was a joke, the punch line to a cartoon. I tugged down my hood. As I walked to the Yeti, I took my out my cell, just so I didn't have to acknowledge anyone's existence. I turned it on and scrolled through my old messages. No word from Pippa.

On the way back, I drove by my mom's place. The *For Sale* sign was still on the lawn, along with the drooping balloons. I pulled up next to the sign, rolled down my window, and grabbed a balloon. Then I untied the string and let it drift away.

The lights were on at Pippa's house. I thought about how many times I'd walked down that block. I was missing that girl so bad, I tried to send a message to her inside my head. Yeah, I knew this was crazy. But I always felt like she was listening.

Please let me know if you're okay.

This silence is freaking me out.

I want to tell you so many things. We never got a chance to talk. I mean, really talk, the way we used to . . . back when we believed in the Wendigo and I taught you the secret language of knots, the way they told stories about rabbits and trees.

Back then, our parents controlled our lives.

They didn't control us now.

I parked on the side of the road. Got out and took a walk to the canal behind her house. The lights were shining in the water. I studied their reflections—what Mr. Bones called "the rule of thirds." You lined up everything in the camera until it looked perfect, the way stuff never does in the real world.

No way could I march up to her front porch and knock. Not after all the drama that went down with my dad. I could only imagine her mom's reaction when the cop drove Pippa home. It made me sick, the more I thought about it.

I couldn't knock on the door. So I did what I used to do in fifth grade. I searched in the grass for the smoothest rock I could find. Then I drew a smiley face on it with my Sharpie and dropped the rock close to shore. That way, Pippa would know I'd been there.

"You forgot to write a message."

She was standing near the water. For once she wasn't all dressed up, wearing stuff that reminded me of a costume. Just her Jack Skellington hoodie and jeans. Not skinny jeans, like 90 percent of the female population at school. And I couldn't help thinking that she'd never looked more beautiful.

Maybe my dad was right. I was an idiot. Because only an idiot would think they had a chance with this amazing girl. I wanted to hold her forever, block out the world and make the bad things go away.

Pippa stuffed the rock in her back pocket. "Bet you didn't know. I saved them all. My favorite one said, *The stars are already ghosts*. Those little messages were so cool, Trent. Almost like song lyrics."

"I suck at writing lyrics."

"Who told you that?"

"Myself."

"You should stop listening to that guy."

"Good idea."

We walked to the front yard, past the rusty swingset. The Yeti was parked a couple feet away. Yeah, it wasn't exactly in stealth mode.

"I saw your headlights," she said. "It freaked me out because I was watching this old movie about a car that's, like, possessed or something. Why are you here, anyway?"

"Does that mean you're not excited to see me?"

"No, I'm very excited," she said. "Oh my god. Sorry. My bad. That sounded really weird."

"It's all good," I said. "Hey, I can't believe you saved those stupid rocks. You could make a necklace out of them."

"True. But I'm allergic to jewelry. Thanks for coming over to rescue me. That's why you're here, right?"

"Any time, homeslice. You know what this means, right? Now you owe me a 'life debt.' That's the samurai code," I said, smoothing her hair away from her face. "What color is this exactly?"

"Ultra violet."

"I might want to dye my hair violet someday."

"That was some serious random." Pippa laughed.

Why couldn't it be this easy all the time? Standing in her front yard, surrounded by all those perfect lawns, it felt like we'd never stopped talking. When we were together, the conversation always picked up where we left off.

"I've been calling like crazy, trying to reach you," I said. "Kind of stalkerish, I know."

"My phone's been out of action, thanks to my mom's insane paranoia. Me and her got into it. It was pretty bad."

She didn't explain more. There were no words to erase what happened.

"Let's chill in the Yeti," I said, folding her hand around mine. "No reason to broadcast this data." I walked her to the passenger side. When we reached the door, her shoulder bumped mine. "Ladies first," I said.

"So do I need a password to get in?"

"Nah. You're a VIP," I said as she climbed in. I scooted in my side, but she was miles away, sinking into her own personal black hole. "Sorry," I finally said.

"For what?"

"For everything. I didn't want you to see that shit."

"Actually, it's not your fault, Trent. Don't even go there. And for the record, I'm not into judging people for stuff they have no control over."

"I know. But your family doesn't act like that. They're normal. I mean, you're so lucky. You have no idea."

"'Normal' doesn't happen in real life. It only makes sense in the movies. Like, if you're driving along a deserted road in a thunderstorm, there's always a motel at the next exit. But it's usually haunted."

"Or populated by axe-wielding serial killers," I said, pushing my seat back.

"Or both."

"The Miccosukees don't believe in curses," I said. "You're in charge of your own life, right? Nothing can mess with you. Not unless you let it."

I wasn't sure if I believed in that stuff. What did I know

about my Miccosukee family? Alligator keychains and beaded moccasins, my uncle's wrestling show for the tourists with their cameras, ready to catch their twenty-dollar glimpse of the real Florida.

"How often does your dad freak out like that?" Pippa seemed embarrassed, asking this question.

"He's never hit me before, if that's what you mean."

"What are you going to do now?"

I looked away. "I don't know."

"You can't stay there, Trent. He'll do it again."

"He was drunk, okay? Things got out of control."

Back when we used to listen for the Wendigo, I couldn't imagine anything more dangerous than a flesh-eating monster. Now I knew the world was so much scarier than any creature I'd shaped inside my mind.

Pippa sighed. "It's pretty obvious you're defending him."

"So what? He's still my dad. What the hell am I supposed to do? The cops don't care. This isn't the first time they've come to his house."

"It isn't?"

I shook my head. "It's usually the people down the street, calling in a noise complaint or whatever. But I guess murderers and drug dealers take priority over drunks." I raked my fingers through my hair. "I'm really sorry. This sucks so bad."

"Stop saying you're sorry."

"I wanted to show you things," I said, tracing her knee.

"You did."

I tipped my face against her neck, inhaling the peppery

scent of her skin. Then we were kissing again. I slid my fingers toward her waist, just resting them there as we held each other. The backyard turned quiet and empty, like something you don't notice until it's gone.

thirteen

She owned me.

If this girl told me to jump into Biscayne Bay, take a flying leap off the causeway, and swim with the sharks, I would have done it. Gladly. There was no way to explain it. I'd been spinning my wheels. Looking for what? I couldn't tell you. Now I was in the safest place I knew. Damn, it felt good, holding her close.

I tugged the zipper on her sweatshirt and slid my hands inside. I wanted to feel her skin. I tilted back the seat as Pippa straddled my lap. She sank down, pressing her hips against me as I shifted my weight and prayed I didn't explode. I tried to concentrate on the seat buckle digging into my biceps, the distant wail of a car alarm toggling between octaves. Anything to keep my dark energy under control.

Yeah, I was losing it.

Big time.

Michelle had never kissed me like that. I don't even

think she liked kissing. I know it's not cool to rate your ex. Don't get me wrong—the sex was really hot. I'm talking off-the-charts hot, like, sex in the key of awesome. But let's be honest. Even off-the-charts sex gets boring after a while, if that's all you've got.

At first, it seemed like Pippa was into it. We were sweating like crazy and the windows were all smeared up. Then she put on this self-conscious act, which I wasn't buying for one second. If you look that good, you have to know it. And the stuff she normally wore was far from nun-like.

"What happened to your tights?" I whispered.

"My tights? I didn't feel like wearing them, I guess. What's wrong with jeans?"

"Nothing. I like you in jeans."

She gave me this hurt look, as if I'd slapped her. God. Say something nice and she takes it as a put-down.

I leaned in for another kiss, but she turned and I ended up with my face in her hair. My usual moves had zero effect. I tried digging my thumbs into her shoulders, rubbing circles around her pressure points—a shiatsu technique I learned from this paperback I'd found lying around my mom's house, *Oriental Massage for Therapeutic Touch.* I'd skip over the New Age garbage about unblocking your chi and flip to the good parts, all those full-color pictures of sleepy-looking girls lying half-naked on their stomachs.

Pippa moved my hands away. "This is getting too intense." Talk about stating the obvious. My brilliant suggestion?

"We could go somewhere. It's your call. Whatever you want to do."

"I don't want to do anything."

Okay.

The front yard wasn't exactly a VIP lounge. "Maybe we could walk around?" As soon as the words fell out, I knew she would laugh.

"Walk...where exactly?" She glanced out the window. Nothing but pavement and the constant push-pull of head-lights. What the hell was I thinking? I felt bad about dragging her into this situation. Pippa was more the stay-at-home and watch-movies-on-demand kind of girl. Actually, that sounded cool to me.

"This Michelle person..." She trailed off.

"You hate me, right? I can totally feel the hate rays," I said.

"I don't hate you, Trent. I'm just trying to understand what's going on."

"I'm not with her anymore, if that's what you mean."

"Really? I didn't get that impression from your dad."

"It's over. In fact, it's been over for like...centuries."

Pippa didn't look convinced. "You're friends then?"

"I've got enough friends, thank you very much."

"Friends with benefits?"

Whoa. I didn't see that coming.

Might as well tell the truth.

I took a breath and let it out. "We hooked up at my dad's house. This was before you came along. Yeah, sleeping with my ex. Probably not the smartest decision. Whatever. It just happened."

"So that makes it okay?"

"It won't happen again. That's a promise."

"You shouldn't make promises," she said. "Not unless you really mean it."

Now I was getting heated. "Come on, Pippa. Don't act so perfect. Sometimes there's, like, no clear line when you're breaking up. Know what I mean?"

Pippa kept staring out the window. "No. I don't."

That's when it hit me. Oh my god. How could I be so dense?

"So you haven't … "

She looked straight into my eyes. I had no doubt when she said, "I'm still a virgin."

The word dangled between us. It sounded weird, hearing it out loud, like from a fairy tale of the Middle Ages, the "virgin princess" locked in a castle. Or a saint who gets burned at the stake just because they believed in something.

Pippa wasn't a saint or a stuck-up princess.

She was the realest person I knew.

She was also really sexy, in the coolest way possible. In other words, she didn't have to try.

"You want to ditch me now? Let's get it over with," she said.

"Why would you think that?"

"I don't know." She twisted her necklace—one of those vending machine prizes made of rainbow candy.

"Did somebody do that to you?" I asked.

She didn't answer my question. Then again, she didn't have to.

"Well," I said. "Whoever he is . . . I'd like to break his face."

"That's kind of unnecessary."

"I'll hold him down and you can go first," I said, punching the air. "We could charge admission. What do you think?"

"I think you're crazy." She laughed.

At least I got her to smile again.

"That guy was an asshole. I can't justify his actions," I told her. "But please don't think all guys are like that."

"I'm starting to believe you."

"Good. Because he didn't realize what he had. Even more, he didn't deserve it."

We hugged for the longest time. It was the kind of hug that belongs in its own category. I didn't want it to end. Then she pulled away and we were sitting in the car again, doing nothing.

"I have to go," she said. "I've got school tomorrow." The lamest of excuses.

"Right. Except tomorrow is already today."

I was still thinking about Pippa's hit-and-run guy. He'd left damage without actually touching her or anything. Call it psychological warfare.

"I'm guessing you're suspended? I mean, are you ever coming back?" she asked, breaking my trance.

School was another dimension. How was it supposed to prepare you for real life? It sure as hell wasn't helping me. Then

I remembered the stupid film project we were supposed to finish together. I couldn't leave her stuck like that.

"Yeah, I have to stay home til Friday," I told her. "It's kind of idiotic, if you think about it. They won't let me go to class because … I didn't go to class. Don't worry, though. *I'll be back*," I said in my fakest Austrian accent.

She busted out another giggle. I loved that she cracked up so easily (whether my jokes were actually funny or not). There were no games with Pippa. That's what slayed me. We always laughed at the same things. When I was little, I used to think girls were special. Now I knew the truth—they were just as messed up as the rest of us.

I was aching to kiss her again, unzip that baggy sweatshirt along with her jeans (in that order). Instead, I was opening the door, helping her out of the Yeti. Maybe out of my life, depending on whether she'd talk to me again. Yeah, it was that awkward.

"Will you text me later?" she asked. "My phone is officially ungrounded now."

"Sure. No problem." God, I sounded like a caveman.

I would chisel pictographs into my body, if that's what it took to communicate with you …

As I walked her across the lawn, our hands swayed and brushed against each other. It took superpowers not to close my fingers around hers. I still couldn't figure out what she wanted. Were we friends? More than friends? I couldn't risk losing her trust again.

"I'm giving you a shout-out on Power 96 tonight," I told her.

"Like, on the radio? People still do that?" She pointed at my Converse. "Your shoe's undone, by the way."

"Yeah. I'm working on it."

Pippa crouched on the pavement and tightened my laces. "You're the one who taught me about knots."

"What about them?"

She smiled up at me. "They tell stories."

"And you believed that?"

"Sometimes," she said, tying a perfect two-loop knot: *over, under, around.*

"Call me before you go to sleep," I said, like I was her dad or something. "I'll send you a text."

Please don't go. Can we just sit here and talk about knots until the sun turns supernova and torches the earth? Because that would be okay with me.

When she reached the porch, I couldn't watch her leave. I looked up at the sky and thought about dark energy. Not everybody believed in it. Some scientists called it a trick. A miscalculation. One day, the universe will run out of time.

Good thing I won't be there.

———

The lights on the Rez speared the cypress trees. I pulled off the highway onto Old Tamiami Trail, a tunnel of darkness broken by houses so packed together, I couldn't tell where one ended and another started. If you kept going down Loop Road, you'd find swimming holes, ranger huts, and trailer park refugees—old biker dudes selling car parts and chicken eggs on their back porches.

The longer I stayed in the Glades, the more I realized that "home" was a place inside my mind. I didn't need a fence or a yard. I was still pissed at Mom for selling the house, but what could I do about it? Jack shit. That's what.

I swerved around the skate park. Kids were hanging out practicing, even this late at night. I wanted to join them on the ramps, but I didn't belong there. Guess I was still trying to figure out where I belonged.

As I rolled past the school, I spotted this kid thumping a basketball against the coral rock walls. He wore a trapper hat, the flaps bouncing as he slammed the ball up and over. I buzzed my window down and shouted at him.

"Nice hat."

He saluted me. "Thanks, Trent."

The kid actually remembered my name. "Can I have it back?" I asked.

"Maybe later."

"How much later?"

"Later."

Little jerk. I was starting to like him.

Back at the house, all the lights were off. I figured Dad was out, but his Kawasaki was parked under the chickee hut. A bunch of tools were scattered like medieval weapons on the lawn. Another "project" he never finished.

The front door was unlocked. Pretty typical for the Rez. Yet I still couldn't shake the creeped-out vibes. I stumbled inside, flipped the light switch, and blinked at the mess in the kitchen: a puddle of yellow grease slicking the counter. Breakfast of Champions. Fried eggs and beer.

Wasn't Dad supposed to be in charge?

Let him clean his own garbage.

I helped myself to a beer, flopped onto the couch, and pried off my kicks. Pippa had laced them so tight I'd lost circulation. What was she doing right now? I couldn't stop thinking about what she'd told me. If I ever met the guy who'd hurt her, I'd smash his brains out.

Yeah, I was a little obsessive.

Did she think about me, too?

Doubtful.

The beer wasn't helping, so I pounded a couple more. Then I got up and stumbled to the bathroom. Right away, I knew something was sketchy. I almost slipped, walking in there. The floor was damp. At first, I thought Dad had taken a shower. He always left the curtain open, spraying a tsunami of water everywhere.

Not water.

The tiles on the floor were spackled with blood.

My stomach clenched. The room smeared as my legs buckled. I couldn't stand up straight, couldn't catch a breath. Normally, I wasn't the kind of person who freaked over blood.

Judging by the color, it hadn't been there long—a red glob, though more sticky than wet. I shoved my foot under the shower faucet and teetered on one leg, desperate to rinse off the nastiness. Then I splashed my eyes, as if that could scrub away what I'd seen.

All around the house, I yelled for Dad. His bedroom was landmined with dirty clothes. The stereo glowed faintly in the corner, a CD spinning inside, silent.

No sign of him.

I checked my room in the back of the house. My sleeping bag was rolled tight, like I was geared up to hike the Seven Summits.

I grabbed my heavy duty Maglite. Might as well check outside. The backyard was thick with mosquitoes. I searched behind the house, where the Everglades spilled all the way to the patio. I stood there, under the chickee hut, and squinted at the "River of Grass."

Where the hell was Dad?

I circled the patio. As I headed toward the house, I bumped against something in the sawgrass. I took a step back, half-expecting to find a gator. They liked to hang out near the canal at night. Instead, it was a pair of legs crumpled on the lawn.

Dad. He was lying facedown, in nothing but his boxers.

I crouched next to him. "Shit."

That's all I could say.

I grabbed his arm, flopped it over, and checked his pulse. I had no clue what I was doing. His forehead was shiny with blood. Maybe he fell in the bathroom? How he got out here was anybody's guess.

Here's the most degrading part. I was too fucked up to move him. I could barely push him onto his side. I racked my brains, trying to remember what I'd learned in Health class—all that stuff about choking to death and swallowing your tongue. Maybe it was too late to try.

God. Please. Make him wake up.

I tugged off my shirt and pressed it against his head. The blood sopped through the flimsy iron-on letters: *Native Pride*. I balled it up and flipped to the clean side, but it darkened within seconds. I needed to get him into the house.

Again, I tried to hoist him under the arms, but it was like wrestling a fallen log. My uncle could drag an eight-foot gator in circles by its tail, but I couldn't move a grown-ass man. The best I could do was whisper at him. Try to nudge him back to planet earth.

"Dad," I said, over and over.

He breathed my name.

"Trent?"

"Yeah. I'm here."

He wasn't dead. At least not yet. I wanted to turn around. Run. As fast as possible. Just leave him there to rot. After what he did to me, there was nothing I wanted more.

But I didn't run.

Lights blared from Uncle Seth's house. "Don't move. I'm coming right back," I said.

God, that sounded idiotic. I started marching toward the lights, still half-wasted, and I fell, more than once. When I finally got to the porch, I must've looked like hell. I couldn't get myself together. I was pacing back and forth in my bare feet, trying to make up my damn mind.

Knock.

Or don't knock.

Near the door was a stack of cans filled with BB pellets. Girls would strap them to their legs to make music for the Green Corn Dance. The girls would spin because the universe spins, the same as everything in it—plants and animals and people, too; the way it always was. The way it always will be.

I knocked.

When it opened, a woman leaned on the door frame. She wore a straw hat tipped low on her forehead and a heap of beads around her neck. Her thighs reminded me of bedposts, thick muscle packed into khaki shorts.

She squinted. "You're Jimi's boy."

Around the Rez, people still called my dad "Jimi."

"You don't look too good," she said, scratching her neck. "You don't smell too good, either."

Who was this crazy lady? All this time, I'd thought she was the girlfriend. Now I wasn't so sure.

"Where's Uncle Seth?" I asked.

"Gone." She steered her gaze to the yard, which ended at a wall of stringy pines near the canal. "No use fussing about it. Can't keep him away from the city lights."

I felt like she was talking to the trees, like I wasn't even there.

"It's the lights that draw young people," she said.

Inside the house, the TV crackled applause. A woman

was screaming, all hyped about winning a year's supply of Cheerios or a trip someplace that wasn't here, one of those countries whose names I memorized then forgot how to spell.

"My dad's hurt," I said. "He needs help. I can't do it by myself."

"It shouldn't be up to you." She shoved her feet into a pair of flip-flops. "Come," she said. As we marched across the yard, her gray-stained braids swung down her back. She was a lot older than I'd guessed. What did she mean, *not up to me*?

When I first moved onto the Rez, I thought I'd have total freedom. Instead, I got roped into Dad's sick version of reality. The knots were yanked so tight, there was nothing I could do to pull myself loose.

Nothing except chew my way out.

fourteen

The room was spinning.

I was tangled in sheets. My mouth tasted gritty, like I'd swallowed a handful of sand. Even the inside of my nose felt dry. I tried to focus on the ceiling fan, but it kept shifting and the bed wouldn't stay still.

In other words, I was seriously fucked.

The solution?

Close my eyes and drift back to Dreamland.

As I rolled over, the blanket snapped out of my grip. I figured it had slid on the floor. I reached for it, stretching my entire arm off the edge (definitely not the smartest move; everybody knows the bed demons have a weakness for dangling limbs).

"Wake up, Trenton."

The bed demons had learned how to talk. They were calling my name. And they didn't sound happy.

"Did you hear me?"

Yeah, I heard you the first time. Loud and clear. *Extra* loud, as if the world's volume had cranked up.

"Aren't you supposed to be in school?"

School? Why start now?

"It's time to get out of bed."

Time is a human invention. When nothing happens, it doesn't exist.

Actually, something was happening.

The woman I'd met last night (not that I'd call it an "introduction") was standing over me. In her arms, she held my jeans, neatly creased on top of my *Native Pride* T-shirt.

It could only mean one thing. I was half-naked, in nothing but my boxers. This was only slightly embarrassing for one reason: I wasn't sober enough to give a shit. Yeah, it was already morning and I was still drunk. How twisted is that?

"Do you remember where you are?" she asked.

To be honest, I didn't know. I remembered the blood on the bathroom floor. All the beers I'd pounded. Me and Pippa in the car. Her body sinking on top of mine.

"I'm not at my dad's place," I said. A brilliant observation.

"Correct," she said.

"Whose place am I at?"

"Mine."

Now I was totally confused.

"Not Uncle Seth's?"

"My son-in-law lives here, yes. But this house belongs to me."

The headache behind my eyes had moved toward my brain. "His wife was your daughter?"

"Granddaughter, as a matter of fact," she said, folding my clothes on the dresser. "Call me Cookie. Everybody does."

I was still trying to register the news. The only grand-mother I knew was my Nana in Fort Myers, the one who loved dogs more than people.

Cookie wasn't like any grandmother I'd ever seen. Her hair was coiled in a long braid, slung over a Harley Davidson muscle tank, and her throat was speckled like a conch shell. So were her knuckles, the same as most old people. But she didn't look old. That's for sure.

"Me and your dad ain't exactly on speaking terms," Cookie told me. "But he finally got you dragged back to your Indian family. I'll give him that much."

"Where's Dad now?" I asked.

"In my sewing studio. Same as he's been for the past month. Wasting time on the wrong things."

"Wait. The Little Blue House is your sewing studio?"

"Until Jimi moved in. Now I've got to make do with the shed. All my beads are still packed away. It's an absolute wreck." She sighed. "If you're not going to school, might as well make yourself useful. Help me move those damn boxes into the house."

I sat up straight. "Is Dad going to be okay?"

"That's his decision," she said and closed the door.

———

Maybe if I hadn't been so wasted, I could've moved that stuff like a boss. Cookie had no problem lifting all those boxes into a wheelbarrow. She made me push it across the yard in the broiling sun.

On the porch of the house was a Styrofoam cooler. I thought about *Fantasy Factory*, that episode where they're riding a cooler on wheels. I peeked inside. It was stuffed with bones. I lifted a gator skull, surprisingly light and grooved with pits. A tooth skittered across the porch. For some reason, I put it in my pocket.

As I grunted and lurched my way through the garden, Cookie stopped and pointed to the chickee hut. "Your dad built it for me. Took him three days just to clean the bark off the cypress."

"For real?" It was one of the biggest on the Rez.

"Got one of them draw knives over there, if you want it."

Dad's initials were carved into the blade. I tried to picture him scraping the logs into those smooth pillars, so tall and wide I couldn't wrap my arms around them.

"When did he build that thing?" I asked.

Cookie lowered her hand toward the ground. "You were this high. Just big enough to get into trouble. You're how old now?"

"Seventeen."

"I don't tell my age to nobody," she said, squinting up at the chickee, where some of the palmetto had thinned out. "Looks like the roof needs fixing."

"Can you show me how?"

She shrugged. "Ain't nothing to show."

We spent the rest of the day in the backyard. I didn't think about Mom ditching me, selling the house. I didn't think about Dad getting so wasted he cracked his head on the bathroom sink and somehow managed to stumble outside, just a few feet away from the chickee hut he'd built when I was little.

"You learn by watching," Cookie said.

That was the *Eelaponke* way—her term for Miccosukee. As we worked, she told me about the beginning, when Breathmaker pulled us from the clay and made all the animals on the earth. The panthers were supposed to crawl out first, but their heads wouldn't fit.

"They couldn't do it by themselves," she explained. "So the bird clan helped them out."

"Sounds like the panthers aren't too big on peace." I stepped off the ladder while Cookie held it with one hand.

"They have a place, same as everything," she said, passing me a Coke. "The snakes and alligators, even the ants, they all have a place."

I popped the tab and took a long sip. Coke always burned my throat going down. In the late afternoon heat, it tasted better than water. I stared off into the distance, where the Everglades unrolled like a tarp. Did the big cats still hang out in the sawgrass? Or were they hunted down and killed years ago?

"Ever see a panther?" I asked.

"Nope," she said. "Just you."

I wanted to ask more questions, but Cookie grabbed the wheelbarrow and pushed it back to the porch. As we packed up the beads, she told more stories about the animals and how the world got started.

"The panthers were Breathmaker's favorite," she said.

"So why didn't he help them?" I asked.

"He was watching, all along." Cookie patted my shoulder. "That thing in your pocket ..."

I slipped a hand inside and squeezed the gator tooth.

She gave me a slow smile. "Keep it."

And I did.

Uncle Seth came home looking like hell. We hadn't really talked since he called the cops, the night Dad went ballistic. At dinner, we made Indian burgers with fry bread. Probably the best thing I've eaten in my whole life. And trust me. Eating is one thing I'm good at. He showed me how to knead the bread. It's all about letting it breathe. Man, I could eat that stuff every day. No joke.

"I'm staying here now," I said.

Uncle Seth took off his straw hat and plunked it on my chair. He was still wearing the baggy patchwork that everybody called Big Shirts, so I knew he'd been putting on a show for the tourists. As he helped himself to a burger, I waited for the bomb to drop.

"That's fine," he said. "But this isn't your dad's place. There are rules."

"Okay. I'm cool with that." To be honest, I would've agreed to anything.

He gave me a little speech about alcohol, how it makes "too much heat" and burns your insides. I was half-listening, half-tuning him out, sort of astral projecting the whole time, but he had a point. I didn't want to end up bleeding in the grass.

"You're going to school," he said. "And you'll still work for me on weekends. Does that sound fair?"

I nodded.

Cookie fixed a plate and wrapped it in a paper towel. "Go ahead and take this over to your dad. He's sick in spirit, not just his body, and that's the way it is."

Crossing the backyard, I thought about all the bullshit he'd put me through—the chalky smell of the blender in the morning, the bottles stacked in the sink like bowling pins, the epic humiliation in front of Pippa, and now this.

When I saw him passed out in bed, all my dark energy fizzled away. He was tucked under a beach towel, like he was only taking a siesta. An Ace bandage drooped off his forehead. Yeah, this was the man who brought me into the world. A freaking rock star.

The stereo was still playing with the sound off. What was he listening to last night? I hit eject and the CD tray slid out. The label, a swarm of magic marker, looked mucho familiar. Here's why.

It was my own crazy handwriting.

The CD was a mix of classic rock songs I'd recorded for "inspiration." Just me and my Gibson, channeling Jimi

Hendrix, the guitar hero who shared Dad's name. That's about all they shared, as far as I could tell.

In my freshman year at Southwinds, I did okay, but I wasn't exactly an Honor Roll kid. The whole concept of school was a joke to me. Alone in my room, I'd listen to Dad's vinyl. I tried to imitate the Jimi swagger, but it ended in failure. That's when I started writing my own songs—so many, I ran out of CDs. I grabbed whatever I found around the house: Mom's yoga tapes, *The Magic of Muscle Singing*. Yeah, I was a little obsessed.

When you give something, you're supposed to get something back. I put the greasy plate of food on the dresser. The .357 Mag was under the bed, locked in a case the size of a lunchbox. I crouched on my hands and knees, grabbed the handle, and pulled.

"You play good. Might want to borrow an amp next time, boy. Improve your sound. Get yourself a 40-watt. Crank it up a little," Dad mumbled at me.

"It's not about playing loud," I said, backing away from the bed. How he could just lie there, giving me shit like nothing had ever happened? I should've been used to it.

Dad sat up and gave me one of those looks. The Nazgul stare. He was sick in spirit. If he wanted to get better, he'd do it himself.

"A damn shame you gave up," he said. "If you'd kept at it ... who knows? You might've turned out better than me."

It was pretty obvious that he saw the gun. Only one thing mattered. I wasn't scared anymore. I slipped a finger inside my pocket. The tooth was still there.

"I didn't give up, Dad. You did."

He nodded. "That could be true, boy. You've got a lot of panther blood. I knew it the minute you were born. That's why I got those papers."

"What papers?" He wasn't making any sense.

"The tribal papers. Got them signed by the elders."

I still wasn't getting it. "You mean, like, adoption?"

"That's right. I got you into the tribe, right when you were born." He leaned back against the pillow. It sounded like he was bragging. Of course, when it comes to Dad, the subject always revolves around him.

"Why didn't you tell me?"

He reached for the plate. Took a big bite and wiped the grease off his chin. "You never asked."

The "heat" inside me was ready to burst. I'm talking a supernova-style explosion, bright enough to eclipse the galaxy.

"How could I ask you, Dad? You weren't around. I used to tell people that you were rocking out on tour. And you know what? I almost believed it. How sad is that?"

"You can believe whatever you want," he said.

If I wanted lame advice, I'd read Mom's books about how "energy flows where your attention goes."

Well, I knew where I was going.

As I turned to leave, Dad started his guilt trip. "You think it's been easy for me, trying to get back in the swing of things here?"

"I never said that."

"Trenton ..." He kept whining. A magic spell to make me listen. But I was done listening.

I wanted a new name.

fifteen

I've never been an early morning hater. The start of the day is a blank page. Anything could happen—maybe the earth's magnetic poles would flip and deep-freeze the school, just in time for the morning announcements. Or maybe a secret volcano, bubbling under the football field, would scorch the bleachers into a Kentucky fried crisp. Of course, there's always a chance of a UFO invasion, though I doubted it for one reason: If aliens were so highly evolved, why would they come here?

On Friday morning, I was trapped in the guidance counselor's office watching my friend, Mr. Velcro, peel the skin off his thumb.

"Gators do the same thing." I pretended to read the magical permission slip that allowed me back in school.

Mr. Velcro peeled another clump of dead skin. "Gators do what?"

"Molt," I said.

He dug inside the file cabinet. "I just spoke with Mr.

Bonette. He says you've been doing pretty well in his class. In fact, he's quite impressed with your analysis paper … "

Unbelievable. Mr. Bones actually liked my film essay.

"He has a lot of faith in you, Trent. Now if only you'd channel that energy to your Language Arts class…" He signed the permission slip and shoved it across his desk. "Can I share my honest opinion?"

Whenever I hear that question, my answer is always no.

"I wish you had faith in yourself," he said.

We moved into the front office, and I glanced up at the TV. It was showing the pre-recorded ads for Coffee Corner. (Don't ask why we needed commercials for something we couldn't buy. The coffee fundraisers were only for teachers.) A little freshman kid dressed like Zeus or Merlin or some old guy with a beard was chanting, "Try our heavenly hazelnut."

"You can always talk to me if you need someone to listen," Mr. Velcro was saying.

Nobody wanted to hear about my dad passing out on the lawn.

Mr. Velcro was still waiting for me to talk. "What do you think?"

"I think I should probably go."

But I had to wait again, for the principal, and I heard Pippa's sweet voice on TV. Another week of band practice and Chess Club field trips (does that sound like an oxymoron?). I thought about her ex, the hit-and-run guy. Did this idiot spread rumors about her? I remembered what she told me. The crank calls, the stares in the hall.

Was it hard to stand in front of that camera and face the entire school?

I took out my cell. Now was the time to send a very important text message:

Talk about the zombies

Pippa squirmed in her chair, but she wouldn't look away from the camera. So I sent it again. And again. Finally, her eyes flicked down to her lap. No doubt checking my text. Then she raised her head and smiled.

"Have you taken precautions for the zombie apocalypse?" she asked the school.

In the guidance office, a herd of freshmen girls were falling asleep in their chairs. At least, until now.

"Oh my god," one of them whispered.

"If zombies attack Miami, we should try to quarantine ourselves," Pippa continued. "You'll want to stock up on non-perishable foods. And maybe a couple gallons of bleach. The Florida water supply isn't what it used to be. Not after somebody had this great idea about draining the Everglades."

Mr. Velcro gawked at the screen. "Is this a speech for the debate club?"

"You're probably thinking, 'How am I going to carry all my stuff in case I need to run?' Well, it's all about recycling," Pippa said. "You could always make a purse out of your Capri Sun pouches. Don't forget. Plastic lasts forever."

Everybody in the front office was glued to the morning

announcements. The freshmen girls did that Transform-
ers-style move of joining forces around the TV, as if they
shared electrical circuits as well as brainwaves. Even better,
they were clapping, although Pippa couldn't hear them.

I wouldn't call it a speech.

More like a manifesto.

———————

It was lunchtime when I finally got out of there, so I headed
straight to the cafeteria, which belonged to its own special category of hell. Along with the usual social drama, there was
nowhere to sit and have a real conversation. Not when you're
lined up like zoo animals.

Last year, my class at Southwinds took a trip to Busch
Gardens. We walked inside a fake cave and stared through a
window at this gorilla named King. It was supposed to look
normal and jungle-like in there, but he wasn't falling for it.
He rocked back and forth, throwing whatever he could grab.
Basically, he trashed the place. When I moved closer, he lifted
his food dish and cracked it against the glass.

As I circled the lunch tables, I knew what that gorilla
must've thought. I wanted to blow shit up. Tell everybody to
stop chugging their artificially flavored milk while I smashed
their goddamn cell phones.

Pippa sat way in the back, surrounded by a wall of band
people. God, she looked amazing. I tried saluting her, like a

complete idiot. She kept talking to those nameless flute girls as if I didn't exist.

I was so confused, I almost jumped when my stupid watch started beeping. For some reason, I imagined the beeps were inside my head, like the government was spying on my thoughts. Yes, I know this makes no sense. It's just how my brain operates.

The smell of burnt grease made my stomach twist. Usually, when I'd been drinking, I'd kidnap the nearest hamburger and hold it for ransom. But I hadn't touched a beer in days. Guess I was suffering from some serious withdrawal.

Enough of this garbage. I needed to talk to Pippa and congratulate her on that badass zombie survival guide. I'd been trapped for way too long in the front office—what a load of bullshit. I would've rather hung out on the Rez and help Cookie with her epic sewing projects.

Only one thing was in the way: Me and Uncle Seth had a deal.

Call me a walking disaster, but I sure as hell wasn't a deal-breaker.

I snuck up behind Pippa and stole a french fry. The last time we talked was in the driveway at her house. Just thinking about it made me sweat. I slid next to her and tried to harness my dark energy back to the present dimension.

"You know, plastic doesn't really last forever," I said, digging through the soggy pile of the fries until I found half an onion ring. I love when that happens. "Of course, the same is true for zombies, even though they're already dead."

She didn't laugh at my stupid joke. Any sane person would've taken the hint. But no. I kept spitting out random information like I'd morphed into a human version of Google.

"Plastic lasts about a thousand years. Of course, this all depends on what kind ... "

While I blabbed on like an idiot, Pippa's backup crew glared. I'm talking major death rays. They got up from the table and finally left us alone. Good. I'm sure they had better things to do, like clean the spit out of their flutes.

Pippa still wasn't smiling. "So what happened to the shout-out?"

I wiped my fingers on my jeans. "What shout-out?"

"The one you promised."

Damn.

"Listen, homeslice. A lot of shit went down. I mean, after I left that night. My dad basically went crazy. I'm staying with my uncle now. He's real cool. And there's a lot I want to show you. There's this gator that Cookie feeds. She makes toast for him and leaves it on the dock."

"Cookie?"

"You haven't met her yet. She's kind of like my grandmother, but we're not actually related. Oh. And I just found out. I'm part of the tribe. It's probably the only smart thing my dad's ever done."

"Wow. That's nice, Trent. And you still had time to go around talking behind my back?"

This wasn't going the way I'd expected.

Pippa crumpled the empty fry packet—the only thing on

the table. She didn't even have a tray. Maybe she was on some kind of carbohydrate diet? In one quick swoop, she beamed it into the trash can.

"Nice shot," I said, but she was hustling away, sort of half-tripping in her Frankenstein boots. I was right behind her.

"Did you think I wouldn't find out?"

She was beyond pissed. Why? I couldn't tell you.

"Find out what, homeslice? I'm not a mind reader. Just tell me what's going on. Can I beat him up for you?"

"Not unless you beat up yourself."

"Me? What the hell did I do?"

"You were at a party with Michelle. That's what people are saying."

"What people?" I already had a guess. Kenzie and the female mafia strike again. "Listen. I didn't invite her to Alvaro's house. She was just…there."

"And why are you talking to your ex-girlfriend? We can't be together if you're still with her."

"But I'm not."

"So you're not with Michelle. But you're sleeping with her. Is that how it works?"

"You've got it all confused. It's over with that girl, okay? Like I said, it's *been* over." I was freaking. How could I be in trouble for a crime I didn't even commit? Most of all, I couldn't stop thinking about the word "together."

Were we together?

I pulled my cell from my pocket. "Look. Michelle's number isn't even in the contact list. I deleted it."

"Your laces are untied. And you dropped something." She pointed.

The gator tooth had fallen out. I picked it up before it got trampled. When I turned around, Pippa was gone. Of course, I started running after her.

I was in the moment.

That's all that mattered.

When I reached the lockers, I raised both arms like I was crossing the Olympic finish line. Pippa was not amused. I shoved my phone in her face, trying to get her to see.

"See?"

Pippa waved my hand away. "You can't erase what happened. Not when it's already done."

"Okay. You're mad at me. I get that. But give me a chance to ... you know. Make you un-mad."

"Too late for that." She dug inside the locker and yanked out her Language Arts book. The cover was wrapped in a paper bag, as if it hid something dirty instead of boring essays about Research Skills. Too bad we didn't read stuff that was R-rated, or at least PG-13. Then maybe I'd stay awake.

"Let me prove I'm not a liar." I checked my text messages. Sorted through the random contents of my life. It was kind of pathetic, especially when absorbed all at once.

I scrolled through, barely paying attention, until Michelle's number popped up. Sure, I'd deleted her from the list. That hadn't stopped her from texting me after I left Alvaro's. I'd been so wasted that night, I didn't remember answering it.

Michelle: Why did you leave so fast?

Trent: Got better places to be

Michelle: That's why you should come over

Trent: No thanks

Michelle: Because of your gf? She won't find out.

Trent: But I found out about you

Michelle: Are you in love with her?

Trent: Yes

The whole situation didn't seem real. I kept staring at the screen. It felt so weird, looking at stuff I had no memory of typing. That's how drunk I'd been, just minutes before I'd found Dad on the lawn. Almost like an out-of-body experience. Or ghostly possession.

I was the ghost.

Pippa had left me standing there alone. Okay. It was too late to erase the damage. I couldn't travel backward in time and tell her about Michelle at Alvaro's. Maybe I could move forward.

The first thing I did was block Michelle's number. No more booty calls from her. Next, I ran up the stairs to find Pippa. It wasn't like I'd memorized her schedule or anything. I still hadn't memorized my own. I must've looked like a creeper, moving from one classroom to another.

The windows in the doors were painted with flying hearts and these creepy-looking babies with bows and arrows. That was bad enough. Then everybody had to take turns scratching bad words into the paint. So it was like "Yay, let's celebrate love. And by the way, fuck you."

I peeked through the scratched-up hearts. It was so dark in the room, I could barely see anything except the dull glow of a television and Pippa's sweet face in silhouette. Guess the teacher was showing a movie. What's the point in coming to school if you're just sitting at a desk, watching some lame DVD that you could probably download for free online? I mean, come on.

Slowly, I cracked the door. A beam of sunlight oozed across the carpet.

"What can I do for you?" the teacher mumbled, like a waitress taking an order at Denny's.

I wanted to say, "You can't do anything." Not a single person on Planet Earth could help me now. It was all in my hands. Instead, I said the magic words:

"I need to talk to Pippa."

All the heads in the room craned around. Pippa was trying to melt into her chair, but she couldn't hide from me.

"Do you have a permission slip?" The teacher was going on about campus rules. Like I needed her permission to talk to the girl I loved.

The stupid TV was blasting a speech about Manifest Destiny. In other words, the excuse to do what you wanted. Take away somebody's home. Steal their food and basically destroy the land. We're supposed to pretend it happened a long time ago. Well, history repeats itself. That's one thing I learned.

I cruised past the teacher and headed straight for Pippa's desk. "Come on," I said, stretching out my hand.

She stared at it. Then grabbed hold.

We marched through the classroom. When we reached the door, she said, "I'll be right back."

I was trying not to laugh. For a second I almost forgot she was pissed. It didn't take long to refresh my memory.

"You better have a good reason for this."

"Trust me. It's good," I said, pulling her toward the staircase.

"How can I trust you anymore?"

"Here's one reason." I brushed my mouth against her ear.

"Stop."

"You want another reason?" I kissed her neck, the warm space below her throat. Both of us sank to the steps. The railing was bubbled with rust, like it might collapse at any second. The whole school was falling apart but I didn't care. We could hold on to each other.

When we finally let go, Pippa said, "I waited for you to call."

I looked at the trash that had rolled, tumbleweed-style, to the bottom—all the deflated snack bags and crumpled balls of paper. At that moment I felt like tossing myself into the pile.

"Yeah, my ex was at that party. I had no control over that. And you're right. I should've called when I got home, but I was too wasted." That's what I told her. The truth.

"That's no excuse," she said.

"No, it's not. But I want you to know I'm sorry."

"Sorry you got caught?"

"Just ... sorry."

Pippa leaned against my shoulder. I held my breath and stayed still so I wouldn't break our connection.

"Remember back in sixth grade?" she said. "You used to call my house in the middle of the night and we'd talk on the phone forever and watch movies and stuff."

Technically, you couldn't watch movies over the phone, but I remembered.

"You never wanted to hang up first," she said, laughing. "I'd say goodbye and all I'd get was dead silence."

"I liked your silence."

"Me too," she said. "I mean, I liked yours."

We sat there, being silent. Then I kissed her forehead. "Don't hang up on me, okay?"

Pippa hooked her thumb around mine. "Promise I won't."

Alone on the stairs, it felt like we were the last humans on earth. That wouldn't be so bad, as long as we were together.

"Your mom probably hated me calling all the time," I said. "No wonder she didn't want me coming over."

"What're you talking about? I thought it was your mom."

We both looked at each other.

There had to be a good reason why our moms broke us up. They probably couldn't deal with our co-ed slumber parties once me and Pippa hit middle school. Or maybe they thought we hung out too much, we needed more friends. Or friends that weren't the opposite sex.

Was there a good reason?

I couldn't think of one.

Pippa was still holding my hand. "Just to let you know… my mom doesn't hate you. Everything's been weird since my parents got divorced. You saw my house. It's not like I'm oblivious to my mom's hoarding problem. I just don't want people to know about it."

"Because they'll judge you?"

"Of course," she said. "What do you think?"

"I think it's time to stop caring so much. All families are weird."

"Feels like it sometimes."

"Well, yeah, trust me. You're not alone."

She sighed. "There you go again with that trust thing."

"Give me a chance. Please. I swear, I'm trying to do better."

"That's what you keep saying." She stood up so fast I almost fell.

As she headed back toward her classroom, I opened my big mouth. Let her know what I'd hidden inside.

"Is this really about your mom? Do you honestly think anybody gives a shit what your house looks like? Or is it more about you, homeslice? And don't try to front like you have no idea what I'm saying. Because you're smarter than that."

Pippa didn't turn around. She stopped near the busted water fountain, the Florida version of Old Faithful. Only it wasn't leaking anymore. Maybe we'd finally drained the earth's natural resources. Not that I'd call the school's fountain "*au naturale.*"

The fountain must've fixed itself. Pippa bent over for a sip and I couldn't help checking out her tights (and the things underneath). She wiped her mouth on her sleeve—a dangerous feat with all those staples.

"Let's finish our stupid film projects," she said. "I don't want to get a bad grade on mine because of you."

I knew what this meant.

It meant filming her mom, the house, and the whole damn mess.

"When can I come over?"

"Tomorrow," she said.

"I'll be there," I promised.

The stairs were still empty. I waited until Pippa had snuck back into class, and then I walked across the campus, all the way to the Hole. It was starting to rain and the trees had brightened, like somebody had turned up the tint in the field. I didn't have any weed on me. No beer, either. Nothing to dull my head. And that was okay with me.

I wanted to swim through the Everglades with Pippa. Make her believe I wasn't a liar. Kiss her under the chickee hut that I would make new again. Feed bread to the gator, who had a place like the ants in the sand. Why would I live anywhere else? The city was speed without a pulse—a world of cars and street signs that glowed but never gave any light.

sixteen

The school auditorium was floating underwater. That's how it felt, the night of the film screening. A mirror ball sprinkled chips of light across the bleachers, where families hunched in rows, taking pictures with their cell phones.

No sign of Mom. I must've been insane to invite her to this thing.

Her response?

"I'll see if I can swing by."

And as I could see, Mom wasn't there.

She used to follow me around with her video camera. She was always trying to capture a moment, as if nothing was real unless we recorded it. Once in a while, her voice would boom over the jittery footage of my birthday parties.

"Give us a smile, love," she'd say. "Come on. I know you can."

That's the weird thing about home movies. They only show one side. I wondered about the parts that get erased. Or the scenes left out, just minutes after it fades to black.

Mr. Bones gathered the entire class on stage. He was standing in the same spot where Pippa had shared her zombie storyboards with me. It was only a few months ago, but it seemed like forever. That's why I liked remembering things inside my head more than watching Mom's old videos. The pictures belonged only to me.

"Listen up, guys. I need a copy of your shot list." Mr. Bones had the whole blazer-and-jeans thing going on, as if this were the Oscars and we might stroll down the red carpet. When nobody listened, he said, "Your final grade depends on it."

Pippa was supposed to be here, but she hadn't showed up yet. I was starting to panic. I glanced at the audience, a blur of nameless faces. You could tell which families belonged together by the way they smiled.

Near the top of the bleachers, Cookie sat by herself. Every strand of her silvery hair was braided. She wore sneakers under her patchwork skirt, but I thought she looked exactly like a queen. While everybody else talked and laughed, she stared straight ahead, not saying a word.

Finally, Pippa came gliding down the aisle. She never ran anywhere. She always took her time, as if the world were spinning fast enough.

"Did you finish the shot list?" I asked.

"It's good to go." She handed the paper to me. At the top, she'd doodled a wreath of stars in magic marker: *Trent + Pippa = Team Awesome!*

"I'm so freaked out right now. You have no idea," she said. "There're so many people here."

"Just imagine them in their underwear," I said, hoisting myself onto the stage.

"I'd rather not."

"Check out the bald dude in the second row. What do you think? Boxers or briefs?"

"Maybe he's got Underoos."

"Hey. There's your mom." I flung out my arm and pointed, as if we'd floated out to sea like a couple of pirates.

Pippa grabbed my arm and squeezed. "What if we totally humiliate ourselves?"

"That's okay. It's one thing if you're humiliated alone. But if you're together, it's not so humiliating."

"Nice logic," she said. "I think I see your grandma. She's sitting way in the back, right? The patchwork lady?"

I laughed. "Man, I can't wait for you guys to meet. Cookie's got so many amazing stories."

I couldn't wait. But in a way, I could. We had time to keep learning about each other. Drive around the neighborhood late at night and sing with the radio. Tell secrets in the dark, like we used to do back when we believed in monsters. There was time for everything, the old and new, along with all we hadn't done.

———

The screening lasted as long as a Hollywood movie. Two hours of Life Portraits. There was the usual "talking head" stuff, even though Mr. Bones had said it was off-limits. Most of the class just put an old person in a chair and filmed them, straight on. They asked the same boring questions:

What's your name?
Where were you born?
When did you get married?
Blah, blah, blah.

After a while, it all blended together. It felt like our existence was only a checklist. Or a series of things to do before you're dead.

When the Everglades swelled across the screen, a woman behind me sighed, *ahhh*. It startled me so bad, I didn't recognize Pippa's "establishing shot" of the gift shop on the Rez.

Some people believe the Glades is just a swamp. They don't understand that it has its own beauty, the kind that finds you instead of the other way around. The cypress trees and the vultures told this story. The missile base, the unpaved road where we'd walked, the fence where tourists hide from sunburns and sleeping gators. Pippa had also filmed a bunch of faces from the Rez: the kids playing basketball, the ladies stringing beads. It was all there, the old and new.

I gave her a hug. "Good job, homeslice."

When I glanced behind us and searched for Cookie, perched at the top of the bleachers, she flashed the biggest grin. I wondered what she thought of the film. Did she recognize our world inside the frame? Mr. Bones said that everybody sees a different film in their minds. It's all about the way our memories get mixed up with the truth. I wasn't sure if I believed him, but it made a lot of sense to me.

The soundtrack played over the credits. My bass guitar chords floated through the auditorium like smoke, reminding me that music captures time like a film. For a moment, it's there with you. Then it's gone.

I nudged Pippa. "Where'd you get the music?"

"The tape was in your car. Remember?"

"Yeah, but I forgot that song was on there. I'm still working on it, you know? It's not ready for public consumption."

"Too late now."

As the credits hovered over the screen, everybody burst into applause. I clapped, too. I didn't stop until my palms tingled.

"You're next," Pippa whispered.

"So you've got psychic powers now?"

"Not really," she said, "but I can recite the alphabet. *O* comes after *M*."

This was it. The entire school was about to see her mom's house. When I'd gone over to shoot the project, I'd told Pippa to wait outside. She had no clue what I filmed. It had taken the rest of the semester to edit it.

While Pippa sat on the front porch, I'd been in the living room, talking to her mom. I filmed her in extreme close-up. You couldn't see the Glad bags behind the couch. Or all the piles of magazines about *Better Homes*.

"My daughter thinks it's Halloween year-round," said her mom-on-screen.

Pippa sank down in her chair.

"She wears the strangest things. But even with all the

Goth makeup … is that what you call it? Goth? Or is that not hip anymore?"

Behind us, a girl snorted.

"Whatever," said Mrs. McCormick. "I still think she's the prettiest girl in the world."

Pippa turned and looked at her mom. A real mom.

My film cut to a series of shots, a bunch of stills from Pippa's family albums. They dissolved from elementary school pictures all the way up to the present, fast-forwarding through time.

"You know, Pippa was beautiful as a baby," her mom's voiceover told us. "And she's even more beautiful now. I don't say it often enough, but I'm so proud of her. Sometimes I forget that she's not little anymore. I just wish that I could hold onto her forever."

In the auditorium, Pippa's mom was wiping her face. It was hard to see, but I could tell that she was crying.

"My daughter has grown into her own person," the voiceover went on. "That's because she takes after me."

The auditorium exploded with giggles. Pippa's mom was actually funny. Who knew?

"You can stop filming now." She blocked the lens with her hand. "Is that thing still recording? Where's the off button?"

"It doesn't have one," my voice mumbled off camera.

After an awkward moment of silence, the film was back in focus. Pippa's mom was still talking in the background, but she wasn't on screen anymore. All you could see in the frame was their parrot, Holmes, his lizardy feet and prehistoric stare.

"I'm trying to teach him a few words…" My voice boomed across the auditorium. It was always strange, listening to myself outside my head. Did I really sound that lame?

Holmes melted away, replaced by a montage of Pippa's room and everything in it. Her collection of vintage cameras. All her Tim Burton movie posters, curled like treasure maps on the floor. I even filmed the Crayola scribble on her bedpost, the letters that spelled her name.

My film was edited like a mixtape, sampling DJ-style and pasting moments in time. When I thought about it, this was an awesome way to make a "portrait." Not one point of view, but many. It was all about telling the truth.

Maybe there was more than one.

———————

After the screening, the whole class got together in the art room. Mr. Bones passed around a star-shaped balloon and told us to sign it. He said we should practice our autographs just in case we became famous. Usually I'd laugh at that sort of BS. Did he really think we would graduate and morph into Hollywood directors?

Mr. Bones was high-fiving a bunch of seniors, telling them "Good job, guys" and all that crap. When he came to me, I expected him to say the same pre-recorded lines.

"Real nice editing, Trent," he said. "Did you use any ND filters?"

"No. Was I supposed to?"

He smiled. My mom would've gone off about the silver in his molars and how the metal leaks into your bloodstream. "Are you going to keep making films outside of class?" he asked.

"Well, Pippa started this zombie screenplay," I told him. "But now we're thinking of doing a music video."

"Something a little less violent?"

"Oh, there's going to be violence," I said, and he smiled again. "Maybe even ultra-violence."

"Viddy well then," he said, like Alex DeLarge in *A Clockwork Orange*.

Pippa grabbed a tray of paint and started mixing the colors. It was nothing but ultra violet for that girl.

"What is this? Finger-painting?" I stole a couple of her brushes and did a little drum solo on the table.

"I'm going to sign it with your blood."

"Sounds like fun," I said, squeezing a tube of Hooker Green. (What was Hooker Green, anyway?)

She passed the balloon to me. It was soaked with signatures in all different shades. There was hardly any room left. I found a spot near the top and signed my initials like we used to do in elementary school, back when we sculpted ashtrays out of clay.

"Your film was pretty awesome," she told me.

"For real?" I kept tapping my paintbrush on the table.

"It was more than awesome. Seriously. You made my house look normal."

"Your house is normal."

"Actually, you made it look beautiful."

"I filmed it like I see it."

We started talking about music videos, our epic plans for the summer. Pippa was going to shoot it on Super-8 and I would edit the whole thing. I really wanted to film my new songs so we could post them online.

"That's how you build an audience," I said.

"Obviously you have it all figured out."

"With our skills combined, we could be a superforce."

"Unless we stop talking again."

I put my hand on her knee. "We're never going to stop talking."

She laughed. "Yeah, right."

"Listen. I refuse to let that happen. You understand? I mean, I can't look into the future or whatever. But when I imagine it, I see both of us. That's the way it has to be."

Pippa was staring at me so hard, I looked away. There was a poster of the Color Wheel behind her head, along with a map of Venice, a city I'd never visited in real life. I wanted to see it before it sank underwater. And at that moment, anything seemed possible.

"Let's hear what the spirits have to say." Pippa reached into her bag and took out her phone. "I downloaded this app called Ghost Radar. It's supposed to pick up supernatural voices."

"Does it ever talk to you?"

"Sometimes."

I glanced around the art room. "Hey, Mr. Ghost. What's shaking?"

We waited.

"Guess he doesn't like me."

"He's just shy," Pippa said. "Hold on a second." She put her phone on the table. Out of nowhere, a voice droned as the screen lit up:

JAM

"That's because you're sweet," I said.

"No, I'm not. And that's been on there a while."

TRICKY

"See? It's definitely talking about you."

"Because why?"

"Because you're a tricky and complicated girl."

"Oh god, Trent. Where do you come up with this stuff?"

"The spirits don't lie."

Pippa scrolled down the list. "Most of these words don't make sense."

"You have to make your own sense. That's the secret to the universe. In other words, the answer to everything."

I was getting kind of deep tonight, even though we were sitting in the art room, drawing our names on a stupid balloon. Guess that's what happens when school ends. You're forced to deal with reality.

The balloon reminded me of the *For Sale* sign at my mom's place. Maybe she and Mr. Nameless had already moved away. I'd spent so much time wishing I could be somewhere else, it was pretty weird to think I wasn't ever going back to my old house. Next year, me and Pippa would be seniors. We were almost free. At least, one step closer to freedom.

When the class met outside on the football field, everybody drifted over to their parents. I couldn't believe it when I saw Mom standing near the bleachers. She'd actually shown up. And she was talking to Pippa's mom like they were old friends. Of course, that was the actual truth.

My mom started walking across the field, sort of pecking her way in these strappy sandals. As a kid, I used to think she was glamorous. Now I wasn't so sure.

"Congrats. You guys were fab." Mom swooped me into a hug. She smelled exactly the same, like the herbs at the health food store, all those dead plants to cure your problems. "I'm really impressed with your hard work. Especially the music in Pippa's film. Was that you, love?"

I nodded.

Mom smoothed my hair with her long fingers. "It sounded a lot like your dad."

"He doesn't play anymore," I said flatly.

"Well, that's a shame."

She pulled me close and I sort of collapsed against her, like I was finally letting go.

Cookie was talking to Pippa. "Hope to see you on the reservation. You're always welcome there." She tied a bracelet on Pippa's wrist. It was strung with tiny plastic beads. "If it don't fit, I can make another."

I knew that Pippa couldn't deal with bracelets clacking

up and down her arms. But the beads fit snug against her skin and stayed quiet and still.

"It's perfect," she said.

"See? You're not totally allergic to jewelry. I knew it all along," I said, making her laugh.

We watched the balloon get passed around. Everybody wanted to hold it for some reason. And when it finally came to me, there was nobody else left.

"Let it go," Pippa whispered.

"Isn't that, like, bad for the environment?"

"Probably. But I can think of worse things. Come on. You're the last one."

"How did I get into this?"

I shoved the balloon away from us. It sort of hovered in midair, then wobbled upwards, gaining speed the higher it got. The crowd cheered, as if I'd done a good job. Everybody raced toward it, like they could actually lift off the field and catch it. Or maybe it was more about running, just for the feel of it.

I tugged Pippa into the parking lot. "Got a surprise for you."

"I'm not sure I can handle your surprises."

"Oh, you'll like this one. It's mine now," I said.

"What is?"

"Take a guess."

The Kawasaki was gleaming under the fluorescent lamps. Dad had repainted it black, my favorite non-color. He'd even thrown in a pair of helmets.

"This one's yours," I said. The helmet was decorated to look like a skull. It was totally badass.

Pippa swung her leg over the seat. "So, where are we going?"

"Anywhere you want, homeslice. You're the boss."

"Does this mean I get to drive?"

"It takes a little practice."

"I can learn."

"Of course you can."

From then on, we would take turns. Pippa learned to speed up, steer right or left, and cruise for long stretches like we did in the Everglades. We would learn other things, too, as we kissed under the mangrove trees and swam naked in water so shallow and warm, the seagrass curled around our legs. I could wait for it, like the egrets dotting the branches, watching us with their wings folded, never making a sound.

seventeen

The fire blazes for the Green Corn Dance. It cleanses as it burns. There's no sense of "now." Just the smoke threading the oaks, their branches thick with ferns that wither and play dead in the rain.

I haven't eaten for days. My head is empty and full at the same time. The medicine people are here. Uncle Seth is here, too. Everyone hunches around the fire—the boys from the skate park and me. We've put on our Big Shirts and jeans. Now it's time to chant the old songs.

One by one, they call us into the circle.

They ask, "What is your clan?"

I tell them I'm a panther.

The medicine people are talking about someone who lived a long time ago. He was a good man who did many good things.

They ask, "Do you want this name?"

It's not the "baby name" Dad gave me. The medicine

people chose a man's name for me to carry the rest my life. If I say yes, I will drink the *assi* and stay awake all night. No sleep. Nothing to eat. Only the music, telling stories about the Breathmaker, whose name means everything.

I stare at the flames and think about the stuff I've done. Feels like it happened to a kid I used to know. I'd drive around, listening to static. Crank it up real loud. When that didn't work, I drowned myself in beer. There was never enough. So I drove a little faster.

It's pretty obvious I was going nowhere.

The smoke rises into the trees. We're breathing it together. The medicine people know I'm taking it real seriously, this name. It's a chance to keep the old ways, while also moving forward. If I say yes, I will leave the childish things in the past. Walk into the sunrise as a man.

I'm wondering if I deserve it.

There was a time when the Everglades was a "River of Grass." We called it *Pahayokee*. We steered our boats through still water. The shape of the mangroves was a map we could follow. We moved south like the blue heron, looking for a safe place.

The farmers tried to get rid of us. They drained the land and torched our houses. They stole our corn, but we didn't starve. We never wanted to fight, but the anger was growing, and so was the blood.

When you give something, it always comes back. The rules are in place for a reason. That's why we face the east, watching the colors shift on the horizon. The morning sky is a fruit that ripens, then is gone.

The medicine people wait for my answer. The man who carried this name was a hunter. He was different from me. During the war, he hid from the soldiers. They got lost, trying to find him in the maze of cypress and tall grass. He held his breath underwater, lying flat as they walked past him.

I've been holding my breath, too. There's a lot I need to get done, starting with the chickee hut, built by my muscle and sweat. I can do so much with my hands now. Play songs on my bass without a pick. Sharpen knives and tie the strongest knots, the kind that never slip loose. Hold the girl I love, her hands fitting into mine.

The smoke finds a way inside me. It clears away the parts I want to forget. I stand closer to the fire, letting them know I'm ready.

Ready to say yes.

Acknowledgments

I am grateful to Kate Lee and Tina Wexler for their encouragement and wise insight, and to my editor, Brian Farrey-Latz, whose vision for this book helped me discover its shape. Thanks also to Sandy Sullivan, Mallory Hayes, and everybody at Flux. Big hugs to the Chappell family, Team 305, Jonathan ("the moon followed him"), Mom and Dad for always being there, and Harlan, who listens when I need it most. I am very thankful to Dr. Bill Rothman, Professor Ed Talavera, and to Ranaria for our conversations about film and philosophy. *Buffalo Tiger: A Life in the Everglades* by Buffalo Tiger was helpful to my research. Finally, I owe many thanks to Houston Cypress (Otter Clan) for showing me the Rez and the tree islands of the Everglades, and for your patience in answering my questions. Your kindness was a gift—and so was my glimpse into that special world.

About the Author

Crissa-Jean Chappell is the author of *Narc* (Flux 2012) and *Total Constant Order* (HarperTeen 2007), which earned a bronze medal from the Florida Book Awards, received a VOYA "Perfect Ten," and was named a New York Public Library "Book for the Teen Age." For ten years, she taught creative writing and cinema studies in her hometown, Miami. Visit her online at CrissaJeanChappell.com.